I t
t

A Lay by
Maureen Duffy

I want to go to Moscow

'I think that if I were in Moscow
I shouldn't mind about the weather.'

CHEKHOV: *The Three Sisters*

Methuen

I WANT TO GO TO MOSCOW

First published in Great Britain 1973
by Hodder & Stoughton
This edition published 1986
by Methuen London Ltd
11 New Fetter Lane, London EC4P 4EE
Copyright © Maureen Duffy, 1973
Printed and bound in Great Britain
by Richard Clay (The Chaucer Press) Ltd
Bungay, Suffolk

British Library Cataloguing in Publication Data

Duffy, Maureen
  I want to go to Moscow.
  I. Title
  823'.914[F]   PR6054.U4

  ISBN 0-413-60460-8
  ISBN 0-413-60470-5 Pbk

O donna in cui la mia speranza vige . . .
Tu m'hai di servo tratto a libertate
per tutte quelle vie.

Paradiso XXXI

One

'. . . life passes and will never come again, and we'll never go away to Moscow . . . I see that we'll never go.'

Do you know where Moscow is? Moscow is never. Peel away the coloured skins of the onion domes, the marzipan layers succulent as the witch's house in the wood that fed Hansel and Gretel, and what will you find at the bulb's core? He knew what there should be, at least the substance: ivory, frozen polished Cornish cream. Perhaps it would be warm to the touch, holding Africa and India and the tropical breath of the lumbering grey beast still in its hard waxy pores. Or it might be walrus cold, a freezomint toothpaste sculpture. The arctic sea elephants tugged at his mind, silvery barrage balloons tethered to the ice, flashing their toothy sabres and cleaning their icicled whiskers. Then he was running again but not with his own legs. In dreams he fled through the forest, the runners of the sled carving Great Western lines through the virgin territory of snow while the wolves leapt and snarled. Ahead was the city if he could make it and make them hear, the men who kept the gates. But they were busy with their fires and wine and blowsy frowsty girls. He cracked his whip at the wolves. Their eyes flashed back at him. He would never do it. The leader bunched his muscles to spring. In dreams you saw everything.

He woke sweating, reassured at once by the familiar dimensions, regulation seven by ten of three paces by four if you didn't stride out, with no room for anything to lurk unseen, only the table and the chair and the bowl squatting quietly in the corner on its matchstick whatnot of a washstand under the artificial Disney moonlight of the pale bulb at the dead middle of the ceiling. It was comforting. After the gaudy hopes and terrors of the dream there was no place like home. You knew where you were. With one eye cocked over the ruckle of thin blankets under his nose he could pick out the mock pokerwork letters on the motto above the foot of the low bed: Home is where the heart is. By dropping one lid and raising the other he could make the words jump on the wall and the crude drawings of a cottage cartoon leap in the air as if it had been peppered with buckshot.

'I can't tell if it's a cottage or a cottage,' Thelma one of the queens from the twos had said, twitching the grey serge jacket round her shoulders like a Dietrich silver fox stole and batting the brown eyes under their heavy mascara of boot-blacking and spit.

'It's what they call a blue peter,' he'd answered.

'You should have "Any Port in a Storm" up the other end to balance it then. Honest, baby, any time you want to play housey-housey with me, mama's willing.'

It had been one of the things he'd had to decide straight off as soon as he knew he was well and truly nicked. After all he was still young enough and strong enough to like a regular ration. Outside it was easy enough to fix up a night and say good-bye in the morning with no hard feelings but inside you couldn't get away. Once you got caught up in the jealousies and scraps you lost your status as a loner. It wasn't the old sailor's philosophy of any port that worried him but the involvement. Those who were bent inside usually played it straight once they got out, though he sometimes wondered if the ones who came back again really liked it better arse uppards and this was the only way they could have it legal and with their tight little society's full approval. But it put you at the mercy of whoever you were shagging up with and he didn't want that; better to keep his own hand on the tiller.

The other need was booze. Well that was all right because he could trade his snout for that since he didn't smoke, though it was terrible stuff. You would feel it, almost see it burning its way down the oesophagus and curdling the stomach lining till it was corrugated and flaccid as boiled tripe. His kidneys must be fluorescent. On bad days his gut ached for bitter, cool and peaty and long as an advert ale.

'You are an intelligent man and therefore I shall give you a long time in which to come to your senses and see the waste you are making of your life,' the beak had droned on with the message of headmasters, company commanders and padres since he'd stopped listening to them and taking what they said for gospel. Now he had time, one-third off for good conduct, say seven years more or less in which to plan. From the moment he'd been sent down he'd made up his mind to sit back and take it easy while he worked out his next job.

Nobody was waiting for him. There was no Dickensian little urchin with his face getting snotty-nosed and raggedy because the breadwinner was doing bird, no missus fretting for a hand on her belly and finding it tougher and colder as the nights passed till she took in a lodger. He grinned at his own self-sufficiency. All he had to do was lie quiet and plan the perfect snatch while they fed and clothed him. He could hear the blood roaring in the ear that was pressed to the pillow, keeping him awake yet reassuring him that he was still alive and as he turned he felt more than saw a flicker at the Judas eye where the screw had passed on night sentry, probably to see if he was tossing off. His own smell steamed up at him from beneath the blankets with its reminder of the sixty bodies packed like pilchards into the schoolroom at Old Town Junior in a juice of grime and sweat, savoury as tinned tomato sauce with its cod-liver oil twang. He had sniffed craftily at bits of him, bare knees and palms metallic with the brown-handled black-nibbed school pen that you had to dip, dip in the inkwell like a drinking bird and that blotched and twitched up the page because you'd been using it for a dart before old Morgans came in, and at his own dropped pants and briny socks. The ironframed desks were waxed with the grease from thousands, generations, of children who'd wriggled and rubbed their skins against them until they could absorb no more and had begun to give back, larding your hands and legs as soon as you sat down in the morning. The walls around him now were like that. He might have never left school for all the difference in the architecture and the rules. The cover fell to over the spyhole. He had watched for it through slitted lids feigning sleep. Now he let them close, safe from observation and the dream that wouldn't come again.

The bell woke him at six thirty, ricocheting from flight to flight of the iron stairs, with screws' voices beginning to sergeant major even through the thickness of the walls. His socked feet felt for the cold floor and his prints Man Fridayed behind him to the washbowl. Cold water numbed his hands and splashed into his eyes making him gasp. He soaped his hands briskly against the hard water and washed his face with a lick and a promise like a cat, keeping one eye on himself in the square of mirror. Then he began to shave, the small nibs of stubble standing up sharp in the cold, tautening the skin this way and that and watching his hands and the sweep of the blade intently. There was no need to begin this day in the life of Jarvis Chuff bleeding like a stuck pig.

He pulled his shirt over his head, drew up the grey slacks and knotted his tie neatly. They were his by right of possession, let to him for a time to inhabit, earned simply by his being there. 'And no reason why you should let a place go to rack and ruin just because it isn't your own bricks and mortar.' His mother stabbed her point home with a loaded brush from the top of the steps. A flour pudding leapt and gurgled in the iron pot, filling the scullery with a smell of washing day that mingled with the alkaline antiseptic of distemper.

Sometimes they had it cold for breakfast with a sprinkle of frosting from the sugar sifter. He could just go a slice of that now. He sluiced the bowl round to swill away the clinging scum flecked with beard into the slop pail so that when the door clanged open he was ready to step out and along to the recess for slopping out. If you got there sharpish the stink wasn't so bad. He was done with the sink and into the karsi almost before anyone else was on the landing. Although he didn't smoke he lit a roll up of the coarse black shag to fumigate the place while he sat there. In the same way that he hung the prison drab over the back of the chair at night and pressed the trousers under the mattress so he had ingrained the habit of one slash a night even with a peter to himself.

'How's his lordship this morning?' a grey figure called after him as he made his way back. 'Nicely thank you.' Buzz, the errand boy always darting here and there on mysterious business made easier by his trusty's red band, mouthed at him as he passed: 'Got something for you later,' and winked. Chuff let a half nod tip in acknowledgement, took a broom and began to sweep. The old whitewash flaked and fell constantly and imperceptibly like a despairing sleet. Every morning you swept up a scurf of it; the dead cells of the walls shed in the night. The whole building was crumbling from the inside until there would be only the hard outer case still standing, housing a silt of ash like moondust or the hot flakes that buried Pompeii.

He made his bed meticulously. Never give them a handle. There was always some bleeder who would fault you if he could. Promptly at seven thirty he stepped down to breakfast.

'You eating all your bread this morning?' It was the man who had asked after his health.

'I might be.' He took a long pull of tea, and spread marmalade on a bare second slice. 'You must have worms, Gutsy, the way you put it away and still get thinner; get them to give you a worm pill next time you're up to see the quack. Here, see how generous I am.' He pushed a slice across the table, took his last and salted it away in his pocket for later. Gutsy snatched at the offered piece eagerly, missed and knocked it to the floor.

'You jogged me.'

'I never.'

'I'll smash your face in, Daft Peter.'

'I never touched you.'

'Screw up!'

A dark uniformed figure came over to stand beside the table. 'What's the row?' No one answered.

'You, pick that bread up. Throwing your food about like pigs at a trough. Whose is it?' The faces stared fixedly at the table. The screw paused, debating whether to make an issue but it was early in the day. Some warmth from his own bed still clung to him. 'Next time I catch any of you wasting good food I'll see you get three days' restricted diet.' Turning quickly he marched off before there could be trouble.

It was the pattern of every day. Either you rode with it or you butted your head against it until you were knocked silly, punch drunk from doing bird. That's if you had anything up top to start with. So many of them hadn't. Looking round the table he ticked them off in his mind: Daft Peter who'd never had anything from his dad's word go, Gutsy who was as starved of grey matter as of everything else as if he was perpetually gnawed away from inside, Boner whose great limbs and pint-sinking capacity had him up on longer and longer stretches; only Cracker hadn't been behind the door when the brains were being given out. He sat there now, his fingers alternately drumming or fondling the cutlery, keeping his hand in he called it, sometimes cracking his knuckles so they wouldn't stiffen up.

'Suppose you got arthritis, Cracker?'

'A terrible thought, mate. That's why I keep in training and that's why I give what I get to the missus to put in National Savings instead of blowing it on cars and such like. One day I shall say to her: "That's it. I'm retired. Pack your bags. We're going to live by the seaside."'

'What, give it all up? Let that lovely touch of yours go to waste?'

'Who knows, I might buy a peter of me own; keep it in the back room and play the numbers on Sunday evening, or then again I might just sit back and tune the telly.'

'I don't know how you've got the patience. Why not just put a stick of jelly or a dollop of plastic putty on the bugger and blow the front off?'

'Then they know you've been when they see it all ripped apart in the morning. My way they don't, not at first, not for sure.'

'How come you're in here then?'

Even Cracker wasn't sharp enough. But after all he hadn't done so well himself. Of course there were the smart boys. There was a table full of them, all done for class crimes: fraud, embezzlement, murder, spying. They kept themselves to themselves though they'd seem to fraternize. You knew however friendly they acted they were putting you down in their heads. They'd tried to take him over, especially when he'd landed the library number, make him one of the aristocrats just like they did outside, but he looked straight back at them and didn't give an inch, not a least crack.

'Don't crack your dial, you might break it,' his mother would say when he sulked and it worked every time: he had to laugh and she'd laugh too. 'I can't abide a sullen kid.' Now he wasn't sullen, just too old and fly and no one was going to jolly him into joining. Not that being a loner didn't have its problems. It was what had got him nicked after all. When you were a loner there was more temptation to someone to grass.

He'd known as soon as he rounded the corner that they were on to him, 'acting upon information received', and dodged back into shadow, down the alley, through the back fence of corrugated iron that had one loose panel some gardens along, and so over the intermediate fences and in at the back door. Shoes in hand he tiptoed through the kitchen and up the stairs in the dark that was tinged with a faint light seeping through the windows from the street outside where they were waiting. His knowledge of the house was a reflex conditioned by a lifetime spent together, so that in summer nights as the old walls contracted it seemed to sigh in unison with him where he lay sweating under the slate roof and now he felt it listening round him. In the front bedroom he reconnoitred from behind the store curtain. They were waiting for something, not ready to pounce yet, for a warrant maybe or for him to come sauntering home and walk straight into it as if he hadn't got the cradle marks off his arse.

There was a little while yet, not much, but enough to tidy up. In the back room he put up the blackout he'd salvaged from the war when it had been his bedroom. He'd had big-head hopes of making it a darkroom when he was eleven and then it had been their hideout to squat in in the candlelight or torchlight if some of the gang had had a good day at Woolies. That's where he'd been when they'd come banging on the door for him the first time. Then they'd had to drag him out from the wardrobe where he was stifling in the dust of old clothes no longer good enough to wear but too good for the ragman. In winter they came out for blankets bringing their coffin smell with them. There was the gas ring he'd used for experiments and for melting down the lead they'd half-inched from the mission hall roof though old rags-'n-lumber would hardly give them a quid for it. They knew he was duck-shoving them but what could they do. Go to the police?

He would need a saucepan. The stairs gave softly to his feet as he padded down and up again. Outside there were three of them now. He lit the ring with a hiss and plop, opened the wardrobe where his mother's ARP hat still hung with her black funeral coat, took up one of the thin bottom boards and began to reach in his hand for the dirty blue wedges with their brown bands. As he carried them over to the flames he caught sight of himself in the long mirror of the wardrobe door, his hands full of fivers, cashier, croupier, bookie, the Count of Monte Cristo with credit unlimited, money to burn and nodded. 'A bit chilly tonight. I thought we'd have a spot of fire.' The face tried out a grin that slipped sideways like a distorting mirror.

The bands broke easily. In small handfuls he held the notes over the spiteful blue flames that licked up in broad yellow waves as they took the paper. Then he dropped them into the blackening saucepan. A hundred went as quick as a Guy Fawkes' rocket flaring and dying. Methodically he worked through the bundles. At a thousand the pan threatened to clog. An old wooden coathanger from the wardrobe served as a poker to stir the black flakes. After a time his eyes became mesmerized by the dancing flames and once, dazed, he found them lapping at his fingers that had forgotten to drop their expensive fuel. The little match girl had struck match after match, he remembered, to warm her blue hands and the soldier had scraped at the tinderbox for a last light. Both had got their wishes. Well he hadn't any wishes, not that wouldn't have to be put into cold storage. He laughed at himself in the mirror. Trust him to be thinking of fairy stories at a time like this, 'Proper sawney you look, maundering along with your mouth open.' It was all fairy tales, everything they told you. Do this and you'll be this and happy ever after.

His bonfire was taking too long. The pan was hot with its mass of charred fragments. The coathanger was scorched and blackened. The first load would have to be flushed away before he could do any more. Softly he crept downstairs again, out into the backyard, emptied the mass down the pan, shaking it so that it wouldn't block the pipe, took the opportunity to water it, pulled the chain and flashed his torch for a second. The water was clear. 'They knew how to design them when this was put in. I've no time for these piddling modern ones that won't take a good size windjammer.'

At the end of an hour he began thrusting the notes two-handed at the ring. Each bundle of ten took twenty seconds to do properly. After two hours he had burnt thirty thousand pounds. His eyes smarted; his hair reeked of smoke. His nails were yellowed and blackened. They would wait until six in the morning to take him, he reckoned. A man pulled from his bed and sleep was bewildered, his blood thin with lack of oxygen, his stomach weak. The three men in the street were succeeded by two others and went off yawning. Still he burnt on, with trips to the lavatory whenever the saucepan was too full.

At last there was only one more bundle. Sick with the smell, he put out the light and the gas ring, took down the blackout and opened the windows to let in the suddenly mild February air, earthy from the moist back gardens under a fine rain. His lungs filled gratefully as if he'd been the one burning. Emptying the last panful into a sheet of newspaper, he drew back his arm and slung the saucepan as far as it would go out into the night over the broken fences and the handkerchief lawns, the ramblers and rabbit hutches, into the waste fringe of the factory yard where there were brambles and convolvulus and a miscellany of discarded crocks. No one would notice it there. The handle would drop off and it would rust away or be used by kids playing among the bushes. No one would know it had been used to burn fifty thousand pounds. He left the window open and closed the door.

Down in the kitchen he stripped and washed the reek of burnt paper off himself, including his hair. The clothes he'd been wearing he hung in what had been his mother's wardrobe and dressed himself again in clean from his skin out. For a few days at least while he was on remand he'd look decent. Then he made and ate a jam sandwich and drank some tea. Outside for a last look round he saw the continued flushings of charred paper had blackened the pan and he spent some time cleaning it. As far as he could tell there was no smell. Inside again he slapped aftershave liberally on his face, neck and hands, slicking down his almost dry hair with it. For a night he'd had money to burn and now it was nearly morning. Finally he crept up the passage and put the door on the snick so that it would give at the first touch but was held in place by a folded five pound note wedged between door and frame. Two others he put in the ornate brown teapot, relic of a long dead great-great-aunt on his father's side, inscribed Sarah Chuff 1876, along with some loose change. One he tore and folded into two spills.

When the front door fell open at the first thunder on the heavy knocker there was a clatter, cursing, boots pounding up the stairs, doors flung open above before the back room door itself was pulled back and he saw the faces blinking in its frame at the strong light. He sat at the table as if he had just finished a meal, a lighted spill in his hand about to touch his after-dinner cigar into life.

'Good morning, gentlemen. Did you want somebody?' He crushed the last of the spill into his saucer.

'Right, Chuff, where is it?'

'Search me.'

'Don't come the comic.'

'Why not. A good laugh never hurt anyone so far as I know.'

'You'll laugh on the other side of your face,' and on through the formalities of charge and caution. 'You'll make it a lot easier for yourself if you come clean.'

'Get some dirty little grass to do your job for you, did you, or is this visit the result of a masterpiece of detection?' He sat on, finishing his cigar.

'Is he always like this?'

'Oh our Jarvey fancies himself as a hard case, don't you, Jarvey?'

'I don't fancy you, that's for sure.'

'I thought maybe you did. You've got a right poncey smell to you this morning.'

'I always like to dress for the occasion, you know that, so when I reckon there's going to be a lot of you calling I splash the airfresh about to clear the stink.'

'You're a mouthy bastard, Chuff. Now where is it?'

'It's another thing I've learnt: never have money in the house when the fuzz calls. It has a funny habit of getting into the wrong hands.'

'We'll tear this place apart.'

'Go on. Don't let me stop you. An Englishman's home and all that. Just don't break anything.'

'Shall we turn it over, sir?'

'Just for the form but you won't find anything. If Jarvey gives you permission you can be bloody sure it isn't here. Still, even he might have forgotten something. Take him down to the station.

He got up and stubbed out the cigar. 'You'll shut the front door after you when you go. We don't want all sorts getting in do we?' They would find the loose board in the bottom of the wardrobe. There would be a moment's hope then emptiness, except for one genuine five-pound note of his own to show Kilroy was there. On his way out he saw the other folded one had slipped or been booted between the coconut doormat and the wall. They would appeal against bail of course, thinking he had it all stashed somewhere and would take it and off. Or maybe they'd be clever and set him loose to lead them to it. So he wouldn't apply for bail. He was going down, he knew, for a long stretch, and what were a few weeks more at the beginning. He could run himself in easy with grub sent in and a few comforts before the real bird began.

For it would begin. He realized that as soon as they got stuck in to the questioning. As long as they hadn't known, nothing fitted together but once the finger was pointed they'd find people who'd seen him board the train or root out some small error; there had to be one. Nobody was perfect. Once they smelled you out they could tailor anything to fit unless of course you had an alibi and that he never had. That was where being on your tod caught you again. No sweet little bird was going to pipe up and sing that she'd spent the evening knitting while watching the box with Jarvis Chuff, even if he'd wanted her to. And they knew it. They knew a lot about him.

'Your trademark was all over it, Jarvey.'

'Once somebody told you.'

'Oh, we'd have come round to it in the end. Slow but sure and a good filing system. Tell us where it is and we'll still make it easy for you.'

'Well I was a bit chilly one morning and a bit low on coal so I used it instead of firelighters.'

'Tell us how you did it.'

'Secrets of the profession. If you're so sure, you tell me.' But there was no way out. Even though a jury might set him free or a judge dismiss the case for lack of evidence there would be no peace. They would hound him continually because not only would they hate to be outsmarted but the thought of the money would sear into them. He would never be able to pull another job while they watched and waited. They would come barging in whenever something looked the least like him and turn the place upside down, and even when it didn't, just to keep him on his toes. But it was going to be long. Jesus, it was going to be long.

'How do you plead: guilty or not guilty?'

'Guilty.' There had been a start from the prosecution, the slam of a book hitting the floor and then silence. He was buggered if he was going to sir the old sod.

They let them state their case, making it as black against him as Newgate's knocker itself and demanding the maximum because of his low cunning and lack of cooperation. This animal defends itself if attacked. The beak asked him if he had anything to say. Perhaps he should have boxed clever. He could have done it too, brought the tears to their eyes with a gallows speech about how sorry he was, how he'd panicked and burned the lot, not put it away for a rainy day as they were making out, how he'd never used violence and if he was given a light sentence he'd go straight ever after, with a hangdog look and his voice not above a whisper but a catch in it here and there.

'Speak up, my man,' the old buffer would say, leaning forward to give him confidence. 'We are here to hear what you have to say.' Hear, hear!

But the words stuck in his gullet so that all he said was, 'No, thank you,' because he'd been well brought up. Then they read him the riot act.

'I see no reason why I should not send you to prison for a very long time.'

*

It was quiet in the library this morning. In a minute Greig-Evans, the Welsh nationalist in for blasting a border road, would be brewing up. He might just saunter along to the washroom for the exercise and a look at the sky.

'You, Chuff.' There was a sudden chill in the room as if the figure in the doorway had cut off the sun. Greig-Evans put a hand behind his back and turned off the gas jet. Stokes was one of the old school screws always on the lookout for niggling infringements, for any attempt to make life sweeter, to turn the place into a 'holiday camp'. 'You're wanted.'

'Oh yes.'

'Jump to it.'

'What's it all about?'

'You've got a visitor.'

'Pull the other; it's got bells on it.'

'I thought you wouldn't be too pleased. Look lively. You mustn't keep him waiting.'

'Who is it? I don't know anyone.'

'Like to keep ourselves exclusive. Well it's someone who's very concerned with your moral welfare. I could tell him it's a lost cause but he gets paid for it I suppose, so it makes it worth his while.'

Either it was a probation officer or some trick-cyclist they'd lined up for him. If he refused they'd put a black mark down on his sheet. Once inside it paid you not to aggravate them to the pitch where they could do you damage, stop your full remission when you came up for parole. He straightened his tie and ran a hand over his hair.

'Oh you look lovely. Come on now smartly. Anyone'd think he was going to marry you.' Chuff stepped ahead out into the air, past the rose garden. Overhead whipped cloud was piled like drifting scoops of ice cream that had broken loose from their cornets.

'He says you used to sing like a lark. There's a pretty picture. Who'd have thought you had it in you. Why don't we ever hear you sing now?' He rang his keys together like handbells. 'Jarvis Chuff in a surplice, all scrubbed and shining.' The last door clanged and was locked behind them. They had passed into the administration block. 'Right, inside.' He opened the door of a small interview room furnished with two chairs and a table. Chuff stepped inside.

A man was standing with his back to the room looking up at the high window, his clerical blacks showing dark green against the light, his hands clasped behind his back. He turned at the sound of the door opening and stepped forward with an anxious smile.

'My dear boy. I came as soon as I found out. I'm sorry it's taken so long but since your dear mother passed away there's been no one to let me know. But better late than never. St Etheldreda's tries to take care of its own.'

It was a fit-up of some sort, but what? Should he play it along? 'I'm sorry, father . . .'

'"Call no man father", my dear boy. This is just a short exploratory visit. I shall call again next week for a more serious talk but I did so want you to know you weren't forgotten. Meanwhile you have your New Testament and I want you to read Acts 12 very carefully. I hope I haven't upset your morning routine too much, though I imagine any sort of diversion is acceptable. I won't keep you and the officer any longer but you will remember Acts 12, won't you?' He nodded to the screw.

'On your way, Chuff.' As they passed the sooty roses Stokes said, 'What was all that about then?'

'Search me,' he shrugged.

'Fancy you singing at St Ethel's.'

'Etheldreda.'

'Eh?'

'St Etheldreda. Me mother used to sing too, at the mission. They gave you a free tea.'

'Runs in the family then.'

Back among the soothing rows of books he found that his hands were trembling and his thighs weak as if he'd just missed running over a dog. Why had he embroidered like that, given the story backing as if he knew what it was all about? The whole thing reminded him of a book he'd read once, drawn by the title *The Trial*, where the poor bugger han't known what he was up for or who he was going in front of or anything, like in a nightmare. None of it made sense. He'd heard of some things but never of them trying to fit one on you like this while you were doing bird. Maybe they were still after the money; this was to trick him into a confession.

'What did they want?' Greig-Evans was asking the same question, asking again because Chuff hadn't heard him the first time. A mug of tea was handed to him, its fragrant steam a reminder of hometime with the teapot and the biscuit tin of broken ends you dunked to a delicious pap, ready on the table and his mother who had just washed her neck and put on a clean overall sitting down for a minute before the big campaign of getting the tea began. Why had they mentioned his mother? It was true they knew every last thing about you, so they'd have it on file that she was dead. Then they'd got some tame padre, briefed him and palmed him off as a prison visitor to worm his way into his confidence. But he was on to them. St Etheldreda's where he'd never set foot was a burnt-out remnant, overgrown with rosebay willow-herb, casualty of a buzzbomb after surviving the blitz proper. It wasn't true to say he'd never set foot in it. It'd been one of the gang's hideouts and once as leader, for a dare, he'd pulled open the door to the crypt and gone down, waiting for the lot to drop on him. There was a big notice warning of the danger of falling masonry. If he was vicar of St Etheldreda's it was of a ghost congregation in a nave where birds and rats nested.

'Christ knows,' he said and took a long pull at the tea. 'Any diversion' the old bugger had said. Well he wasn't that desperate, in fact if anything it made him angry. He was doing his time so they should leave him alone. He'd thought that inside he'd have the chance of a little quiet study and here they were trying to stir him up. Maybe that was it. Maybe they thought that if they kept after him he'd give in, tell all in return for a bit of peace. They'd have to see then who could hold out longest and he knew who it'd be. Jarvis Chuff.

'Stop staring into the fire, Jarvey. You'll make your eyes weak.'

'I'm practising will power.'

'If you had as much will as your mum you wouldn't need to practise. I reckon she could bend iron bars just by looking at them.'

'What was she like, Dad, when you first met her?'

'She was a brahma of a woman. Why she ever took up with a rabbitty little bloke like me I'll never know.'

''Cos you wasn't just all mouth and trousers like the rest of them,' she'd answer.

'Dad why aren't you in the army?'

'Oh, listen to him. "What did you do in the Great War, Daddy?" Because he's more use to them here.'

'It's a restricted trade, gas fitter. Anyway I'm C3.'

'And don't ask what that means or you'll get a thick earhole. Why I had to have you last instead of our Madeleine I don't know. So I could be plagued with whys and wherefores in me old age I suppose when I might expect a bit of peace.'

'You're not old, Mum.'

'Listen to him smarming up to me.'

He hoped Madeleine was giving eye to the house.

She'd let it to a young couple on condition they didn't decorate it or mess it about. The things he didn't want them using had been locked in the back bedroom. He didn't want to come out and find it like a tart's boudoir or a motorway steakhouse. He wanted it just as it was, just as she'd left it.

Dear Jarvey,
I have to tell you your Dad passed away very peacefully last night. The funeral is Wednesday. Madeleine has been a great help. She has a new boyfriend, an American sergeant. Work hard at school and be a good boy and we will soon be together again when this wicked war is over. Let me know if there is anything you want. Enclosed 10/- is for pocket money. I hope you still have some sweet coupons to spend it on. Remember me to Mrs Willet and behave yourself with her.
  Love,
    Mum.XXX

He'd done as she told him more or less. Somehow he passed the scholarship without really noticing and found himself in the local high school. Then it was VE and bonfires and he was going home with a transfer to their mixed grammar and for a moment everything in the garden and house was lovely until he began to wake up.

*

The rest of the day passed almost as usual. At eleven forty-five they were marched off to dinner, the hall clanging with the metallic din of hundreds of men messing together, each either shouting to lift his words above it or giving up to shovel his grub as fast and noisily into his face as possible. The air sang like telephones wires in a wind with small tensions. He wasn't in the mood to sit back and observe. With every glance from screw or lag, every least deviation or intrusion, he wondered what they were up to now. He must stop or he would be suspecting everybody, and that way they could drive you barmy, he remembered from their briefing about being taken prisoner in Korea. He'd decided the easiest way out of that one was not to get caught and had once spent hours till dark playing possum among the bits and pieces of the rest of his patrol who had walked into an ambush. Lying with the corporal's hand still clenched around a grenade two foot from the end of his nose he stared as he'd stared into the fire and prayed that no conscientious gook would put a bayonet into him or a pistol to his head. The rest of the corporal was scattered along the track they'd been following. Only when night dropped mercifully over him did he let himself creep into the thick vegetation and retch and weep until he was recovered enough to make his way back to base.

The afternoon dragged busily. A new intake meant a lot of new cards, repetition of direction, the usual requests for books on the Index, some innocent first offenders, some old lags, try-ons, stamping out, tidying the shelves until tea-up. Each one he scrutinized for a plant. But why should they bother? He was nothing, cypher zero, tucked away out of sight and mind behind the fifteen-foot walls. Even for that amount of money they couldn't think he was worth trailing forever.

For a moment he considered dodging the class this evening but then it might look as if he was rattled. No, best be cool; act his usual self. As a rule he didn't hold with going to classes; it showed too much willingness to conform and play the good boy. Some of them as soon as they were sent down started scribbling and daubing away for dear life, learning languages as if they were off on a Cook's tour next week and swotting away for 'O' levels for all the world like kids at a boarding school. They let the system and the boredom con them into forgetting that outside it was all different, that school-leaver's French was bugger-all use to you in a production line or the dole queue. But he had to do something to keep his wits from rusting up so he sat in on, rather than attended, the diploma course in history.

And a fine old whitewash job it turned out to be. 'History as she is rewrit,' he said one week in discussion.

'Ah, Mr Chuff, do I detect a whiff of Marx?'

'I shouldn't think so, not unless he'd got Spencer with him.'

'What's your objection then?'

'It's hard to put a finger on really, just a general feeling that it's all cockeyed like the leaning tower of Pisa and that if you accept it for straight up then the rest of the world's askew.'

'That sounds more like metaphysics to me than an historical objection.'

You couldn't blame the tutor, he supposed. He was only handing out what was dished up to him like those birds that fed their chicks on bits they sicked up themselves. Very nourishing no doubt and it made sure you grew up just like mum and dad and nothing nasty every got stuck in your young gullet. He thought he was doing good coming there week after week, particularly when he had to deal with a thorn in the flesh called Chuff and the only way to fix him was to cosh him over the bonce with a word he didn't know and then he'd lie quiet for a bit. Yet all the tutor did really was prop up the system, make it workable, explain it away by his bland presence and his words so that you couldn't hit back. You were allowed to dance about a bit, make a few fancy passes at authority like a good sparring partner, but if you suddenly upped and slung a hook right to the champ's jaw they were all climbing into the ring to pull you off.

'"They", Mr Chuff? Who are the ubiquitous "they"?'

'Society, authority, the fuzz, the screws, bankers, school-masters . . .'

'We are all "society" surely?'

'When they let us be. Nothing personal of course, but why should you be there and me here?'

'I don't see what that has to do with history.'

'Everything. That's what history's really about: why you're

up there and I'm down here. In the last analysis that's what it comes down to.'

'History isn't to be interpreted in such personal terms. It's a matter of trends, influences, processes.'

'But on the end of them it's just people doing and being done to. Gallipoli was Churchill's mistake.'

'Even if we allow that it was a mistake for the sake of argument, there are very few Churchills in a nation or an era who have the power to make decisions.'

'That's what's wrong then.'

'That's anarchy, man,' Greig-Evans chipped in. 'If we all did what we want . . .'

'You did what you want that's why you're here.'

'That was a representative political act on behalf of an oppressed minority, the Welsh nation, not an anarchic piece of self-indulgence.'

'That's how Churchill would justify his carve-up. My point is why should it only be the Churchills who make the decisions, who do the telling? Suppose I don't want to be told? I'm up before a firing squad or slung inside.'

'It's for the good of the majority . . .'

'Cobblers!'

And so on endlessly week after week while the tutor struggled to inch the march of time forward. You had to admire the way he kept coming back for more. Tonight Chuff wasn't in the mood but the tutor began with a smile, his glasses flashing as he looked along the table, 'Now, Mr Chuff, something special for you: Russia in the eighteenth century. Catherine the Great. What can you tell us about her?'

'She was a murderous bitch, like all the rest of the Russian royals, but a lot less than some and she was a lot less religious with it. But then she was really German not Russian. She fancied guardsmen.'

'Who doesn't?' Thelma whispered from the end of the table.

In his dreams he sometimes felt there was someone else in the sled but he couldn't see who, wasn't even sure who with the given knowledge you have in dreams. Perhaps it was a woman, Catherine the Great herself. The tutor was passing a book round the table with a picture of her. It was a heavy-featured sensual face with regarding gaze to match. The style of the portrait gave her a deep full breast and white plump shoulders. Mentally he loosed the strings of pearls that diademed her hair and let it flow over the shoulders. Then he slid his hands over the white flesh to the low neck of the dress and pulled. He felt himself beginning to stir under the table, the muscles in his throat and at the root of his tongue contracting, and swallowed hard, pushing the book on to the next man. Jesus, if a picture could do that to him he was in a bad way, and of a woman dead for nearly two hundred years. They'd have to come for him with a strait-jacket soon. He began to say the nine times table in his head and was glad the session had long enough to run. Thelma would be offering to help him out again. Nine nines are eighty-one, ten nines are ninety, eleven nines are ninety-nine, twelve nines are a hundred and eight. He took a deep breath and listened to the tutor.

The session over, there was time only for cocoa and bang-up. He had come to like the dark bitter liquid with its reminders of chocolate spread and the NAAFI after a patrol. The piece of bread he had salted away he dunked, sometimes adding a sprinkle of sugar from his supply. Tonight he was glad to hear the screw approaching down the line, the clangour that meant the day was nearly over and there would be time to think. When it came his turn Chuff was standing with his back to the door looking up at the window and the arched ceiling above. There was a moment's pause. He could feel the screw's eyes at his back probing. He stiffened himself for the slam of the door and when it came didn't jump out of his socks as he was meant to do. The lock turned. Still he stood with his back to the door, knowing there would be a face at the Judas eye. He gave it a counted thirty seconds to be gone and turned. It was blank; the cover fallen back into place.

Rummaging under the bed he found the New Testament where he had tidied it away when he had first been allotted this cell. Then he unfolded his blankets and made the bed so that it was more comfortable to lie on. Being an old lag made you an old woman or a tramp. Now what had the padre said, Acts 12? He propped the thin pillow against the head and leaned against it while he tracked down chapter and verse, the lesson for this evening. I am the vicar. Here beginneth . . .

At first he couldn't see that it might have to do with him.

The second verse told about the execution of James. Was it a threat to come after him? Then it all became one story: the imprisonment of Peter and how he was sprung by an angel. He closed the book quickly and put it under the bed. He was sick and sweating. What the sodding hell was it all about? Somebody was trying to get at him, he was sure of that now, and they were fucking well succeeding. He roamed through a blacked-out tunnel cracking off curses like snapshots in the darkness, blinding and sweating until he fetched up smack against the end and there was no way out. For a time he lay there in a dazed heap. He wasn't to be left in peace, slopping out his bird year after year until they had to let him go and he stepped out a free man with a neat tailored plan to begin again. Slowly he gathered himself together. Right then, if that was how it was going to be he must put his mind to work and get a jump ahead. Reaching down a hand he felt under the bed, took up the book again, found the page and began to search the words for clues.

Unless the beginning was some kind of double threat, do this or else off with your head, the chop like James, he could probably discount it. No, it was Peter who had the message. Someone was offering to spring him. The padre must be the angel. Now what about that damsel named Rhoda? Maybe she was going to be laid on for his comfort. Still it was no good if she wouldn't open the door. He was getting carried away, making dream-stuff out of it. And that was just what they wanted of course. First they get you rattled and panicky, then they let you begin to build on it, dangled it in front of you, a near-naked girl on a golden swing in fishnet tights and a rose. There was a bint called Rhoda in his class at Old Town Junior. She was very dark-haired and -eyed, the sort who'd give you a look for a halfpenny or two toffees, only there wasn't much to see when they were nine. There's been another Rhoda too, another dark-haired but burnt-almond-eyed number when he was on leave in Pusan.

He'd be climbing up the walls if he went on like this. No one'd need to give him a bunk-up; he'd be over the top like Spring-heeled Jack and sprinting up the road with his tongue hanging out. He went over to the water jug and poured himself a mug of cold water. Even the nine times table wasn't going to help. Nine times was just about what he reckoned would take the edge off it. It was a pity he'd never taken up yoga. Maybe if he stood on his head a bit and let the blood rush to his brain he might be able to think more clearly. Why and who, that was what he had to decide and twelve nines were still a hundred and eight.

Supposing the bloke in the clericals wasn't a vicar at all but some old Kiter, or up for a touch of the archbishop, that they'd offered a pardon to to trap Jarvis Chuff. There was no one on the outside he could think of would want to do him that kind of a good turn unless the Mile End mob thought they were doing him a favour. That would mean they also thought he still had the spoil. They might be after a cut-in. In fact they could be the ones who'd set him up in the first place. Maybe it had gone like this; one of the mobs, probably his local, had got wind he'd done the job, given the fuzz the tip off and were now offering him out for a fifty-fifty split. They didn't like him going it alone in what they thought of as their manor. Everybody wanted you to join.

It was all a big laugh. Their faces would be a picture if he took their offer and then told them he'd only got two Jacks left in the teapot and one under the doormat. On the other hand it might be Madeleine thinking she was doing him a favour. She'd been awed, when she'd come to see him after the trial and the full details had been in the paper.

'Did you really do it, Jarvey?'

'It said so, didn't it? I pleaded guilty.'

'Yes but knowing you you could have said that just to be different, just to be big.'

'And get a stretch like this? You'd need water on the brain to be as big-headed as that.'

'Have you still got it?'

'Walls have ears and some nasty little insect in blue might be earwigging on us.'

She lived in a jerry-built semi in Basildon, married to one of the office juniors she'd picked up as a typist who was paunching now as officer manager and got his exercise mowing the lawn at weekends and driving the two commercial cute kids round the safari park. They didn't often mention Jarvis over the Kelloggs but sometimes his brother-in-law would feel himself pleasantly jostled by real life when he thought of having a villain in the family and slash at the dandelions manfully on his way to the station in the morning.

Even for twenty thousand quid though, he didn't think Madeleine would risk what she had, unless some menopausal madness was making her greedy for the fleshpots, the Bahamas for the rest of her life. On balance Jarvis decided he could cross his sister off. That left the old rozzers themselves. It was a pity words went out of fashion. That term had seemed a good one while it lasted, with its associations of stropping a razor and cut throats generally. Christ, it dated you though, like a bird's hemline. When he was a kid they'd been just cops or bluebottles. Maybe it was the first sign of middle age when you couldn't keep up with the cant.

Weariness was making his head swim now. Whoever they were they had stirred him up like a wooden spoon in a goldfish bowl and all the thoughts were finning as fast as they could just to stay in one place, not to be whirled round and round in the muck silting up from the bottom so that nothing was clear and he caught at things, images, as they swirled past, only to find they were either empty shells or coloured gravel more ornament than use.

What could they hope to get out of it anyway? That he would lead them to the money. That's what they all wanted and it gave him a great lift of delight to think they were all wrong. But there was no way he could use it. He had decided right at the beginning that the only way was to sit out his time with full remission for good conduct. Anything else would have him running for the rest of his life, rocketing through the dark, with the wolfbreath at his neck and the gates shut in front. He would just find out who it was, say a polite no thank you and watch their faces fall. He was going to enjoy that. What could Pusan Rhoda's real name have been? he wondered as he drifted down to sleep. She'd been bloody good. Nine times nine.

A week and a day later he was summoned again. That was good psychology, he had to admit as he was marched through the flower beds. All yesterday he'd waited, jumpy as hot fat in the pan until by bang-up he felt like an old dishrag wrung out and hung over the tap to dry.

'The reverend Raphael,' the screw, not Stokes this time, said chattily.

'Yes, it would be.' Chuff had spent a few spare moments in the library brushing up on possible names for angels. 'I don't rate a Gabriel, not being a virgin.'

'You know the one about the pregnant nun?'

'She knew it was St Michael because he had it on his underwear.'

'Sounds more like a saucepan lid to me, Raphael.'

'They all are.'

'What?'

'Angels.'

'You've slipped a cog, Chuff.'

'Well, a vicar's a sort of guardian angel, supposed to be anyway,' he retrieved quickly. 'No doubt he's hoping to save my soul.'

'Poor daft bastard. In you go. This one's closed.' He opened the door into the interview room. 'I'll be just outside, sir, if you should need me.'

'Thank you, officer. I'll knock when we've had our little chat. Do sit down, my boy.'

Incongruously Chuff sang in his head. 'Got a date with an angel,' then said aloud, 'I wish they made them girls.'

'What, my dear boy?'

'Angels.'

'Ah, I see you've read your text as I suggested.'

Chuff hoped he would keep to doubletalk. The screw might have an ear to the door and he didn't want to shop anyone. On the other hand if it was a fit-up the room might be bugged to a recorder for use against him. He would have to box clever. 'It's not the sort of reading I go much on.'

'My boy, I am here as representative of a higher power, one which offers you true freedom and a fuller life.'

'Yes, but what does it want in exchange. You don't ever get something for nothing in this life, padre, you know that.'

'All it asks is your heart and service.'

'All? What about something for the collecting box?'

'I'm afraid your years of selfishly following your own path

have made you cynical and suspicious. There are no financial strings attached to the kind of freedom I offer, only those things I have mentioned.'

'Well, I don't want it. I'm nice and quiet here thank you very much and I really don't want to be bothered.' That should upset them if they were listening in. 'You see I'm not really a believing sort of person, more of an atheist, so I don't think you can help me.'

'That really makes no difference. If the call comes there's no resisting it. Remember Saul on the road to Damascus, overpowered, struck down in a moment and carried away.'

It was a threat. Perhaps he had been right in his first thoughts about the chopper for James. The Reverend Raphael continued, 'Once you are summoned it's truly better not to resist. If you resist the higher power when it calls, then you find yourself imprisoned for eternity with no remission and "the stranger shall inherit thy dwelling".'

Chuff clenched his hands and almost stepped forward. He fought down the impulse to knock the ridiculous little man into kingdom-come or the middle of next week, whichever was the more permanent. There was a wild singing in his ears and it wasn't the heavenly choir. 'Piss off!'

A black arm with a soft white hand was held up deprecatingly. For a moment Chuff expected him to say, 'Tut, tut,' but the pursed mouth controlled itself, forced the curve of a smile and said, 'I realize you must feel like a child struggling in vain against his father's loving arms. A certain resentment is natural. But I am not dismayed. If you will reflect you will see it is useless to struggle. You are an intelligent man, otherwise I should not be here. I shall come again next week when you've had time to think.' He rapped on the door. 'Good-bye, my dear boy.'

Dazed, Jarvis let himself be marched back to the library, for once not even noticing the bellying sheets of washed cloud hung out over the yard.

'Man, you look as if you've seen a ghost.'

'It's my ghostly father. He's making it bloody hell for me.'

*

Now the days lost all sort of decorum. Where before they'd plodded, ticking off months towards release, now they were either ripped off, crumpled up and thrown away so that at the end of each he couldn't remember anything he'd done or said, or else they dragged with the slowness of a painful death so that the minutes assumed the visual shape of waterdrops caught by slow-motion camera. The helterskelter alternate swoop and hold-up made Jarvis feel constantly sick as if his mind was all at sea in a force nine gale.

He could get no nearer to identifying the Reverend Raphael's higher power even though he worried at it constantly. The figure in its black clericals grew and shrank as his thoughts veered. Sometimes it was high and menacing; at others it was almost chubby and benign. Even as he sat in the recess cubicle with the bodiless serge dropped around his ankles, Rodin's thinker in drapes, he heard the bland voice telling him not to struggle as if his very bowels weren't his own any more. What was that about shutting up the bowels of compassion? No doubt the Reverend Raphael would like to convince him he could do that too on behalf of his higher power.

By the end of a week he was as exhausted as if he'd really been subjected to the worst the yellow peril could do. It was blackmail, psychological warfare, and they were winning. On the Tuesday before, he gave in. They would be prompt this week, no making him stew for a day and the realization that he knew this much, was that small, not so much jump as hop, ahead, decided him. His peace was gone. He would play it their way and use it to suit himself. If he refused to cooperate they would let it be known that he had been contemplating a break. He would be put into the patches of an escapee, harried and watched, and probably his remission lost. They, whoever they were, would see to that. Hadn't they insinuated a man inside to get at him? If they were after the money they were in for a nasty shock and he might find himself wrapped in concrete or an old carpet, with a hole in the heart that no surgeon would be able to put a few stitches in and cobble together. On the other hand if it was authority trying to get the money back, the last laugh would be on him as he foxed and feinted with a pile of ashes long gone down the sewer to the sea. When Stokes came for him on Wednesday morning for his weekly visit his legs hardly trembled.

'You getting confirmed or something?'

'Confirmed in me evil ways.' Even for a front he wasn't letting Stokes think he was turning holy.

'Maybe he fancies you; you know what vicars are.'

'Oh, I'm too old for that. He likes them before their voices break.'

'What's the pitch then?'

The soft hands clasped ecstatically. Really he was like a telly parson. Maybe he was hired by the hour complete with costume. 'I'm so glad, so very glad. "Cast your bread upon the waters and it shall be returned to you an hundredfold".'

'I hope the Lord is going to take care of his own that's all.'

'Have no fears. You are safe under this benign and all pervading power. "Trust and obey" as the old hymn has it.'

'Personally I'd rather it was a young her.'

'The prison authorities have kindly allowed me to bring you some cigarettes. I know you don't smoke but I'm sure you'll find them useful for barter or something. I hope their being filters doesn't decrease their value. You see I know all about the prison currency and tobacco barons.'

'I'm sure.'

'I don't know whether the officer outside should examine them first.' He produced two packs of twenty still in their cellophane wrappers.

'We could even offer him one?'

'A charitable thought. The first one out of the pack would be courteous. Au revoir, my boy, until next week.'

'And then you'll tell me the deliberate mistake?'

'We must try not to make any, deliberate or otherwise.'

As Stokes trudged him back to the library Chuff took out the first packet and stripped off the cellophane cover.

'Want a fag? The old bastard gave me a couple of packs.' He pulled the little plastic tag and extended the packet with the round white muzzle thrust foremost asking to be taken. Stokes' fingers closed round it. 'Don't say I never give you nothing.'

'I'll put it away for later.'

'That's right. No smoking on duty. They might think I'd been trying to bribe you. Tuck it behind your ear like a grocer.'

'Even when you're being half-way nice, Chuff, you're a snide bastard.'

'I took it in with me mother's milk. It turned green every time she saw a copper. It's what they call a formative influence.' He looked up at the ornate towers of the prison city, a grimy caricature of a travel poster for sunny Italy, at the tidy knitting of barbed wire, the floodlights, the cliff wall and thought it had better be a proper bonza of a scheme to get him out of there.

Again he had to wait until evening bang-up before he could inspect the packets. Whatever there was must be in one of the fags themselves under a filter, according to the padre's instructions. As he leant on the cell doorway, framed in the jamb with his mug at the ready for cocoa, he found himself humming under the influence of that evening's class which had continued the life and times of Catherine the Great:

> 'I will come and find you
> Break the chains that bind you
> Where the River Volga flows.
> You will surely bloom again
> My lovely Russian Rose.'

Perhaps that was what he was trying to do in the dream: sail an eternal convoy through the arctic night to Archangel so that the Axis, he saw always as a massive doubleheaded Thor's hammer, wouldn't lie heavy on that great white body of Mother Russia. On the classroom wall was a map of the world with pinflags they advanced and retreated with the news. Multicoloured, with a great deal in shocking Empire red, the map had one vast acreage of driven white heavily pocked with swastikas, the prints of vultures in the snow. Now the newspaper headlines smouldered with the phrase 'scorched earth policy'. How could you burn the packed ice of the steppe with its entombed mammoths deep down where the light filtered amber and viridian? Movietone and Gaumont British News showed him in smudgy pictures that looked as if they had been wept over; women standing in the snow, bundled in yurts of clothing, heads scarved, close-ups of glittering tears frozen on their cheeks while smoke plumed and billowed around them and the commentator's voice staccatoed the crackle of flames. He wanted to ask his mother if she would burn their house but it was a daft thing to put in a letter. 'London's burning, London's burning' they tossed the catch in singing lessons while he wondered if the other vaccies were saying, 'No it's not,' fiercely in their heads as he was and crossing their fingers against bad luck. 'Pour on water, pour on water,' the last sounds trickled comfortingly.

'You've got a head like a ragbag, full of bits, and all you ever made of it was a mat for people to wipe their dirty boots on,' he said to himself in the square of mirror.

It had been deliberate choice as he had watched Crawler Edwards bumsucking his way up. They had gone to Old Town Junior as vaccies together, passed for the high school and been repatriated to neighbouring streets when the war ended. Chuff had followed Edwards' metamorphosis with surprise and contempt. They had both crawled out of the mud up the reeds into the sunlight still in their pre-adolescent ugliness. Then gradually Edwards' skin had split and sloughed and there had stepped forth a dragonfly. He had gone off flashing his showy rings. With even greater surprise Jarvis saw him sometimes when he joined those round the television in association, the pearls dropping from the fine lips, the eyes magnified by scholarly glasses that only enhanced the immaculately tailored image as he was pithy about economic structures and the philosophy of growth. Not a trace of the mud clung to him. All of it had been washed away by the cleansing processes of education, a social sauna that left you pink, invigorated, a new man. Whereas Jarvis was a pond creature still. They would say he'd been unable to split with his skin at the right time; had refused the benefits offered to him or he would be where Crawler was. One thing he was sure of. The bleeder would never be, could never have been whatever his circumstances, where Jarvis was now. The contrast between his own reflection, prison soiled and crumpled, in spite of all his efforts, and that on the lit screen, precise as a piece of engineering could be, only convinced him he was right.

Maybe the decision had been made before he consciously took it. Maybe his mother's fierce genes had taken it for him. Crawler was made of sponge cake inside that sopped up everything he was told and turned him out a walking trifle.

Jarvis felt himself filled with her sultana pudding where the fragments of her talk hung in heavy suspense. Sometimes it made him feel dull and soggy and at others rich and solid so that he could do anything. Chuff on duff, he thought, or life's ever afters.

The prison library had a book on insects where he pursued his comparison with Edwards, fitting it to what he remembered of school certificate biology. He himself was probably a stonefly which the book said didn't fly very much or very often but came up from a mud nymph like a dragonfly. Sometimes he wondered if his loner's life, punctuated by lengthening stretches of bird, had made him a bit touched or whether if you could open up the thousand or so heads that topped the uniform grey-serge bodies around him and let in a window to each you would observe thoughts as bizarre as his own behind all the observation panes. The light that made its way down from the high windows, together with the low wattage of the bulbs, gave the whole place the effect of being underwater, a sunken liner with its decks and iron staircases where anonymous shoals of grey mullet eddied.

Standing with his back to the eye he examined the cigarettes in the first packet. God send he wouldn't have to pick them all to pieces to find what he was after. He decided to try one from the opened packet and if that proved a dud, one from the other. It should be towards the end of the double row at the back. Which end? A spec of red in the whiteness of a filter beckoned to him with a signal as unobtrusive as a blink. If you hadn't been looking you wouldn't have known it was there. That was the one he would try first.

Taking it out carefully he examined it for tampering. Something, but he couldn't have said what, made him sure this was it. With finger and thumb he pinched the filter from the top of the fag, pushed the remainder down and closed the box, keeping the cylinder in his palm. It was time he changed position in case some screw was blacking his nose all this while and wondered what he was up to. As he turned towards his mug of cocoa his eyes skimmed the door for a flash of the cover but there was nothing. Jarvis picked up his book and mug and stretched out on the bed.

Under a fold of blanket his fingers probed at the filter while the other hand held up the mug. When he had sipped he took up the book and brought his fingers out into the cover of its pages. The filter was in two parts: the top a small host of white sponge and another section which was missing. In its place was a minute concertina of fine paper which unravelled to a strip of nine inches long and half an inch wide. There was just room for three lines of close typing.

The seasickening motion of his days continued. Sometimes the hours blurred like railway tracks under the wheels of an express and he was hurled towards the escape hatch, at others they sat becalmed as though the day would never come. What should be his final meeting with Raphael seemed a curious let down.

'Are you ready to take the big step?'

'As ready as I'll ever be.' They still had to cover their intentions in this motley for fear of a last-minute cock-up.

'Have faith, my dear boy.'

'Yeah, I know. It can move mountains.'

For a moment he held his hands out in front of him but they were quite steady. The iron stairs clanged warningly as he ran down to join the stirred antheap in association. Already card games and board games were being set up. Prison chess made him shudder. It built a prison within a prison, a game within a game. Its rules and characters were the world outside in little. If you played cunningly, learnt the moves and kept your head you could win by locking up the other man. Pawns were expendable, easily knocked off and gone into oblivion while the big guns battled on. Even to set yourself to abide by its rules, its black and white, its hierarchy, seemed to Chuff a giving in. Tonight he could have kicked the boards over as he passed. 'Don't play their game,' he wanted to say.

Already the sky was draining towards dark. At any minute one of the ever-present tensions among the scurrying horde would flare up into a focus of interest and let him slip through the unlocked side door of the plan along a section of corridor and out into the yard in the shadow of an angle, through the rose garden to the library where he would find a key in the door. Raphael's higher power had smelt out a bent screw and leant him in Chuff's direction with a bit of dropsie. The chance came. Voices raised themselves at the end of the hall. All eyes swivelled. Jarvis turned the handle at his back and slipped through. A few quick steps took him out into the air, his alibi on the tip of his tongue in case he should be stopped, but there was no one about. Breathing shallowly he reached the library door, closed his fingers round the cold iron key, turned it and was inside still clutching the key. The sound of shoes on the path and voices made him hold his breath. Soundlessly he inserted the key in the lock and turned it with a click that seemed like an axe falling in the quiet, but the feet and voices went on and presently he saw the combined shadow pass the window farther along, black against the only faintly luminous sky.

His absence from class would be noticed but it would be assumed that he was either in his cell or had chosen to watch the box. No one would worry about him until bang-up except for those who saw him go, and if by chance they didn't he could just imagine the screw when he found he'd gone missing, hopping about like a fart in a collander. With a hand held out before him he crept across the library, daily familiarity making the going easier. His night vision was adjusting itself and he could soon make out shelves and tables in his way. It was quite dark now and he wondered how the time was getting on.

'How goes the enemy?' his father would say and snap up the silver lid of his fob watch. They would come for him at a quarter to eight when the locking-up-for-the-night confusion was at its height. Suddenly the window grew lighter and the objects in the room took on sharper dimensions. The floodlighting had been switched on.

He reached the locked door that was never opened at the far side of the room. At first it felt as if it wasn't going to ever again.

'Come on, you bugger, move.' Then the key bit and the tongue slid back. He passed into the tower that flanked the building which housed both the library and the Roman Catholic chapel. The unstirred air was musty. Chuff began to climb the stone steps that wound upwards. In here it was quite black with a thickness that lay on his face like soot. All sense of time and space abandoned him in the freefall of complete dark. He couldn't tell any more whether he was climbing or descending. His only contact with reality was the narrow wedges of stair that held his feet and the curve of wall where he barked his spread fingers. Nightmare climbed behind him and waited in front. Only the key, warm and slippery now with his sweat, kept him going with a promise that he could get out. Surely he was nearly at the top. His legs ached with the strain of feeling for each step and his breath came painfully and shallowly in the bad air and the fright. Now the key was thrust out in front of him to find the door at the top. Two more turns and it struck against wood. Chuff stopped, moved a step up and tried to control his breathing and his thudding heart.

With his other hand he felt out the shape of the door, its handle and keyhole. Like banging a bird in the dark, he thought to give himself heart, and he'd never cared much for that, though some of the birds preferred it. Bringing his hands together he guided the key in and turned. By some quirk the lock was less stiff and moved easily. Pushing down the urge to drag the door open at once Jarvis wiped his palms on his trousers and then pulled gently until there was a two-inch crack through which cold air streamed in on him, washing the soot from his face. He breathed deep. The air was slightly acid: bird droppings. Or should it be alkaline? Doing bird lime, time ladies and gentlemen, please. He couldn't half go a pint. Shut up, Chuff.

For all he knew it was a positive aviary out there and if he thrust himself among them the whole lot would take off, screeching at full stretch of their beaks to give him away. Best open the door gently. The hinges might be rusty and add to the warning chorus. There might be bats too but they'd at least be quiet. How long had he got to wait? he wondered. He risked poking an arm through the doorway, turning it so that the light through the stone mullions fell on the watchface. No bird noise flurried off at this intrusion. The hands stood at five to seven. Jarvis inched his way into the tower room. The floor was littered with twigs, fragments of mortar and splodges of caked lime. Suddenly a small body hurtled flapping past him so that he gasped and ducked. But there was only one and one wouldn't give him away. Now he felt safe to move more freely. He crept over to the mullioned slits and looked down.

From his position, standing back a little so that no one looking up by chance should catch a flicker of white face, he could see most of the citadel on that side, with a bird's or god's eye view. Foreshortened figures moved about in the wash of floodlight. The screws on gate duty stood together, stunted in their black uniforms and flat caps. He could make out the trees' faint etchings beyond the wall. A lit tube train rocketed by towards Shepherd's Bush. The bulk of A block heaved itself like a wallowing hippopotamus across his line of vision and all around were the bizarre fairy towers of a sadistic Walt Disney built by the prisoners who would live in their fantastic shadow. For a few seconds he hated humankind that had dreamt up such a mockery. Then he turned to the other side, to the dwarf-size slab of oak that led on to the narrow walkround and its wider openings on the night.

He wouldn't go out until it was time but it was as well to have the door ajar ready to duck through. This lock was stiffer again but gave in the end. He had to squat down to it like Alice in Wonderland trying to get into the garden. It opened below the level of the embrasures which were shoulder high. Chuff took a quick shufti through the gap. The space was very narrow but enough for him to stand in. Tired he sat back against the cold stone to wait.

Five minutes before time he got up and reconnoitred on both sides. The scene had barely changed except that someone, Raphael's higher power maybe, had repositioned the toy lead figures. A prisoner passed across the yard with attendant screw. He hoped they wouldn't be late. There was a high-pitched buzzing in his ears of nervous throbbing blood.

Or was it? He strained at the sound, willing his drums not to vibrate. It might be a train. But it was getting louder, no doubt of it, and settling into a recognizable staccato chatter. Chuff scrambled through the hole and stood up just as the helicopter came rollicking over the fringe of trees, chirring like a huge cricket. At that moment the lights were killed, except for a strong beam that reached out from the aircraft to play on

Chuff's tower as the giant metal insect homed on him. He thought he heard shouts from below but he couldn't be sure.

Now it hovered above him, out of sight but chattering angrily. A rope snaked past his waving hand. He drew it in, locked the harness around his body and pulled himself up into the embrasure. The rope tautened steadily, lifting him free from the tower and up as the craft rose. He swung in the cold rush of air as it began to move slowly away. He was in the park, working himself up higher and higher on the swings till the earth and sky changed places. Better not to look down. There was nothing to see anyway. The search-light beam went out. They had cleared first the wall, then the trees. The helicopter picked its way almost gently across the open land behind the prison. Behind Jarvis there was a sudden brightness. The lights had gone on again. There would be pandemonium with all the prisoners making the most of the excitement. Maybe some would try to have it away after him. The screws would be kept too busy to worry about Chuff. He steadied himself against the rope trying not to spin on the end of it. The ground was rushing up before him; now more slowly as the chopper cut its rate of descent to lower him gently in the corner of the common beside the railway.

A few inches from the grass Jarvis unclipped the harness and slid down. At once the aircraft rose and began to scythe away, the great blades hissing through the air. Jarvis ran across the few yards to the kerb where a car was drawn up with its engine running, opened the back door and threw himself along the seat. The driver let in the clutch and pulled smoothly away.

'Get changed,' said a voice from the front. Chuff pulled on a pair of trousers over his own, dragged on a short fur car coat and fur cap, and a scarf round his neck. 'Ready?'

'I reckon so.'

'I'll pull up on this corner. Come into the front.' The car drew up under some trees. Jarvis flung himself into the front seat.

'Nice evening,' he said. 'You must be Rhoda.'

She looked at him in the half-light. 'You'll do.'

'Thanks very much. Where is this?'

'It's a lane for courting couples.'

'Do you come here often?'

'Only when someone drops in. Shall we go?'

The car ran under the trees. He saw her reach forward and switch on the lights. She swung the car round back the way they'd come, out on to the road and towards the lighted windows of the high street swarming with traffic and people. A copper in the white strip of point duty waved them on. Jarvis felt himself sweating under his furs. He hoped he didn't stink with fright. A wilting sickness engulfed him so that he had to hold on hard to his gorge and his wits.

When the spasm passed they were already heading west towards Harrow. For a few minutes she drove in silence. Then, 'Better?' she asked. 'If you want a drink there's a flask in the glove compartment.'

He leant forward, took it out, unscrewed the cap and poured a tot into it. In his weak state he wouldn't risk choking on a swig. It poured through his veins with the force from a broken dam.

'Have another!' Chuff did as he was told.

'She wasn't like this in the book.'

'Who?'

'Rhoda.'

Two

'. . . later on, others like you will come,
perhaps six of them, then twelve, and so on, until
at last your sort will be in a majority.'

'Don't think me rude,' Chuff said, 'but could I ask where we're going?' The brandy was making him feel better.

'You can ask.'

'But you won't answer.'

'I'm only supposed to drive.'

'Suppose I said I wanted to get out now? Thank you for the ride and all that, and your friends for the trip round the gasworks, but I think I ought to be getting home?'

'You wouldn't. You're too intelligent.'

'You mean I wouldn't have a chance: the house'd be staked out and I've got no money.'

She nodded while concentrating on the road. They were still heading west. He looked at her in the street lighting. Well-educated birds, not that he'd had much to do with them, always made him feel nervous and aggressive as if the spuds were showing in his socks. Her dialect of English sounded almost foreign. Crawler Edwards had taught himself BBC speech, beginning by parroting the masters at school. This was way beyond that, as distinct as a brogue or Welsh singsong.

'Don't you think I should know where we're going so that if anything went wrong and we had to split up I could make me own way there?'

'Why don't you just lie back and enjoy it, like rape. Nothing can go wrong, not yet. This is the easiest part. The police will still be wondering where the chopper went, not looking for a car with two people driving out to have dinner in a riverside restaurant.'

'I like the sound of that but I don't know that I'm really dressed for it. Was the choice of clothes yours?'

'Partly. I thought of the hat. No one has hair that short these days.'

'You're not afraid?'

'Of you? We checked; you're not the violent type.'

'That's professionally; privately I might be different.'

'I think I can take care of myself and if I can't I might enjoy it.'

Jarvis was aware of a faint drift of perfume above the apprehension of his own smell of fear. This was a real cool bird. She had him dandled like a baby, jigged up and down to keep quiet whenever he opened his mouth to shout. Yet at the same time she was plucking at him so that he wanted to stop the car and lay her on the cold February grass at the roadside there and then. Must be the nearly two years in stir, two years without it, the excitement and the brandy making him so randy for a bitch he hadn't even seen in full in the daylight, just a voice dropping come-hither words in the warm interior of the car and a whiff of scent.

'You sure you wouldn't like me to drive?'

'Not this time.'

'I'll get a bit of shuteye then, if that's all right.' Jarvis leaned his head against the cold glass of the window and half closed his eyes. He could see which way they were going but the losing conversation was cut off to give him time to recover. Never in all his born natural had he been so out of control of himself and his life. Nick was a Butlins by comparison. A wave had come galloping across the bay when he was just placidly paddling in the shallows, knocked him down and roared out to sea with him on its back while he shouted and floundered and went down for the third time and couldn't call his arms and legs or even his breath his own. Since Raphael's first visit he, who'd always prided himself on being in charge no matter what the outside world did to him, was a hooked fish. Leaning against the chill hard reality of the glass Jarvis struggled for control as the fields and charcoal shapes of tree and hedge unreeled. The house in Thaxsted Road seemed distant, lonely and accusing. Perhaps he would never see it again. Even if he knocked on the door a stranger would open it. To be on the run was to be stateless as well as homeless, fluid and unstable. Chuff was dissolving in his seat like a Boots powder in milk. His mouth remembered the cinder taste of the human Bob Martins his mother had ritualled him with every Friday night. If they took him back now he would have to serve out his full time. If he didn't do that the house was lost to him forever. Perhaps he had made a mistake in being sprung. Looking through his drooped lids at the woman beside him he couldn't believe that they would have carried out their threat to frame him as an escapee. It was bluff and he had fallen for it.

The car left the main road and began to follow its high beam through a narrow tunnel of tall hedges and starless sky. Some way back he had seen the county border sign flash them into Oxfordshire. The townee in Jarvis was always surprised at the sudden depth of rural England so close to London as if the city were the centre of an enormous Ealing studios film set for the Archers and the inhabitants a crowd of rustic extras paid by the day. Madeleine didn't often invite him to Basildon but when he did go, usually at Christmas, he felt himself as exposed in the tidy flat lanes as if he were naked and couldn't wait to draw the streets round him again. Now he felt if he wound down the window there would be owls and cocks calling and god knows what other livestock snorting and whiffling in the dark. A strong effluence of dung invaded the car.

'Makes your hair curl. No wonder they're so brown in the country; kippered by the smell of it. Are we nearly there?'

'I thought you were asleep.'

'The turn-off woke me,' Jarvis lied.

'Another couple of miles.' The big white Rover ghosted on between the hedges. A small svelte shape flowed through the double beam of the headlights, pausing a moment to flash its own green lamps at them.

'What was that?'

'A weasel I should think, or perhaps a stoat. It's hard to tell.'

'As long as it isn't a wolf.'

'Not in these woods, at least not any more. Foxes perhaps although they've mainly left the country for the suburbs where they can live out of the dustbins and not be hunted.'

'It sounds like a cartoon: Mr Fox Goes to Town.'

'I don't know how long people will find it amusing,' she said and swung the car off the road down a steep drive circling some piece of statuary Chuff couldn't properly make out in the dark. The house itself was low and steep-roofed, a main block and two facing wings. Light chequered the gravel from small lead casements. The doorway would need ducking through. It was a cottage in appearance but a mansion in size. There was the skeleton of creeper wired up to the façade and, no doubt, roses round the door in summer.

'Cosy kot on the grand scale,' Chuff said as the tyres slurred in the gravel courtyard. Very close a slightly cracked bell intoned a half hour. Rhoda switched off the ignition. They got out, slamming the doors into the thick country silence. 'Aren't you going to put the car away somewhere?' His voice which he'd tried to keep low croaked like a nightbird.

'I'll leave it here. Sometimes the best disguise is the most conspicuous and people in the village are used to seeing it.' She looked at him across the bonnet. 'You must be hungry.'

'A bit peckish.' He didn't mention that he'd had his last meal of the prison day and wouldn't have been expecting any more. 'Must be the country air. But then so must you. You've been doing all the work.'

She led the way round the end of the west wing, through a wicket and a garden too dark to assess, to the back of the house where more light fell on a flagged walk: the tradesmen's entrance for Chuff. A back door opened into a carpeted passage leading to the hall where a broad shallow-stepped curving staircase in age-darkened wood took them up to more passages. 'This is your room.' She opened a door. 'I expect you'd like to wash and change. Come down as soon as you feel like it.' The door closed behind her. He had been too dazed and embarrassed to try to thank her. Anyway thanking wasn't done. There was nothing you could say that didn't sound put on and it would only embarrass the other side because what could they say back? So you nodded and smiled a bit and both backed away as quick as you could.

Looking round at the room he decided Madeleine would have really gone for it and that it was probably perfect if you liked that sort of thing but it was a glorified dwarf's house from Snow White, all chintz curtains and Windsor chairs. The floor was polished wood with slip mats. A door off, he soon found, led into a bathroom with lavatory. That was a relief. He didn't fancy traipsing about a strange house looking for the karsi. The fittings were all pink. Chuff peed gratefully admiring the low level flush. 'Wash and change,' she had said. He opened the fitted long cupboard and found suits, then the chest of drawers, and took out pants, shirt and socks. Another drawer had a thick white poloneck sweater. He would wear that instead of a jacket. The car coat he hung in the cupboard, noticing that it was imitation not the real McCoy.

Should he have a bath; wash off the prison stink? They had showers in the nick every night if you wanted one but they didn't clean you like a bath and anyway he'd never been one for the jollity of all lads together even when he was a kid in the army. There was too much chance for someone to pinch your arse. As far as Chuff was concerned there was only one good reason for taking your clothes off with someone else present. He locked himself in the bathroom and stripped away the prison drab.

Everything seemed to have been thought of: soap, big pink towels on a hot rail, enough aftershave, talcum powder and deodorant to make him pong like a beauty parlour. He squirted green pine foam into the bath, ran the water to fluff it up and lay down. It was a pity Rhoda hadn't offered to scrub his back. Lethargy enveloped him with the warm suds: he was drifting away in his effete English sauna. Or she could come in with the birch twigs and tickle him up a bit. Hastily he sat up and soaped his armpits.

Ten minutes late, dried, dressed and smelling like a lily he was combing his hair in the mirror. To be perfect he should have had a shave with the brand new tackle thoughtfully provided but there wasn't the time or inclination. He had cleaned his teeth though. Somehow he didn't want Rhoda to get the idea his breath smelt. Funny how your own dial in the mirror never seemed to belong to you. It might as well have numbers and hands instead of features, it looked so dead. He scowled it into a semblance of life. Then he sucked in his cheeks to give the classic hungry lantern jaw. 'Chuff off,' he said to the deadpan deadbeat in the mirror. That was it. He was tired and hungry with tension and booze on an empty stomach. But the bathroom was a warm pink embrace he couldn't drag himself away from to face the strange music downstairs. 'Shoulders back, lad. Get weaving.' 'Yes sir.' He saluted himself, opened the door and switched off the light.

Voices came from a door on the left at the foot of the stairs. Chuff knocked as gently as he could. There was immediate silence and then a voice calling, 'Come in.'

The room seemed to be full of people he didn't know until the Reverent Raphael stepped forward. 'Ah, dear boy, there you are. Now let me introduce you: Princess Haflinger; Mr Chuff; Miss Cracknell, Major Cracknell; Philomela you know.'

They advanced their hands one after the other. The princess had a soft pink one much like Raphael's, Miss Cracknell wrung his hand as if it was a chicken's neck; the major stumped forward on his stick and put out a dry, frigid paw of brittle bone and leather. Philomela merely smiled.

'We are just about to watch your news bulletin on the television, Mr Chuff,' the princess said. 'Phil dear, get Mr Chuff a drink. Shall we all be comfortable? If you could just switch on the set for us, Raphael,' They all took their places, only Chuff still standing, stymied for what he should do.

'What would you like to drink?' Philomela was smiling at him again. He followed her to the sideboard where there were bottles and glasses.

'If there was a whisky that'd do fine.'

She selected and began to pour, her hand steady, smooth fingers about the hard bottle; lucky old bottle, Jarvis envied. 'I take it you don't want anything in it?'

'How did you guess?' He took the glass wondering if he only imagined the slight warmth from her hand. Behind them the voice of the newscaster broke into the room.

'. . . reports the escape this evening from the maximum security . . . serving a sentence of ten years for . . . train robbery . . . fifty thousand . . . never recovered. Circumstances of the escape . . . for part of the unrecovered . . . police believe . . . already left the country.' Jarvis looked at his own face in the reproduced mugshot with total disbelief. Raphael switched off the set.

'Splendid, my dear boy. It really couldn't be better. Just what we wanted them to believe. And all carried through with your usual aplomb.' Jarvis thought of the near panic in the sooty tower; the wave of sickness in the car. Would Madeleine have seen the news and what would she think? He laughed now inside, looking round at the ageing well-fed faces, to think how he had wondered if she might be responsible. But then who could have dreamt up Raphael and co.? Unless he was really dreaming and would wake in his cell or even in his own bed in Thaxsted Road for who could tell in the midst of it when such a crazy dream might have begun. Toasted cheese sandwiches for supper might do it. 'Mum, I had ever such a funny dream.' 'What did you dream? My bum was a lemon and you was sucking it?' The harsh surrealist suggestion that chopped off any further revelation as surely as the axeman at the Bloody Tower.

'You see,' Raphael was saying, 'we know all about you.'

'I've heard that before,' Jarvis took a pull at his whisky.

'What Raphael means Mr Chuff, is that we made a careful study before we approached you to make sure you were exactly the person we were looking for and now I'm sure we were quite right. You must be starving. Some food first and then a council of war as Alex would no doubt like to call it.' The princess took his arm. The major snorted a little and began to stump after them with Philomela while Raphael followed up with Miss Cracknell. They crossed the hall to a facing door and processed into a laid and lit dining room. 'I do hope you like the clothes we chose for you. I'm glad you picked the white sweater for this evening. It's so much better to be informal when meeting people for the first time and I do think white suits fair complexions so well,' the princess chattered on. 'Now if you'll sit here beside me.' She began to wave them to chairs, reminding Chuff of Madeleine's wedding reception or the anniversary and Christmas gatherings with aunts, uncles and cousins to be disposed round a table with both leaves out. There were wine glasses he noticed hopefully.

Hungrily he tucked in to everything put in front of him and was relieved that there was no paraphernalia of a waiter in penguin suit, only a stout body who brought in the dishes and gathered up the dirty crocks. Soup of an unidentifiable kind was followed by a main course of mince, stuffing and vegetables. Then came a custard glass of cream, sherry and a brown jam he thought might be mashed up chestnuts. The princess kept filling up his glass from bottles of chilled white wine. From time to time he took a quick butcher's across the table to make sure he was using the right weaponry.

Philomela/Rhoda must be a sort of secretary-companion to the princess. She was wearing a brown figured velvet dress with full lace collar that reminded him vaguely of a choirboy. But the figure was full and lush and her poise belonged to the great film actresses Dietrich, Signoret, Mercouri. Funny they should all be foreigners. You're nearly sloshed, Chuff. Unobtrusively he hoped, Jarvis dug his fingernail into his left earlobe. There was still a slight sensation but he would have to pull himself firmly together.

Aside from himself, Philomela and Raphael, the rest must be pushing seventy, if not over the top, but they were all very spry. Even the major with his stick stamped and snorted like the old warhorse he no doubt was and showed few signs of fading away. He'd seen such people on the screen but never thought they really existed any more than the 'lawks-mum' skivvies who ran round after them. Here they were though, all sitting up and taking notice, somehow larger than life by contrast with the antheap he'd just left, and flushed with the wine. The princess for instance had shining white hair, skin that was soft and smooth as a baby's bum and almost navy-blue eyes. She must have been a charmer as a girl, still was, in fact, as she led the way back to the televison lounge, leaning a little on his arm.

Eagerly he supped at the coffee though he knew it would keep him awake. Even Nescafé could do that at night and this was made with real beans, he thought, thick enough to stand a spoon in not like the froth of the coffee bars. It made him shudder as it went down but it seemed to be doing the trick.

'Now, Mr Chuff, I expect you're wondering what all this is about,' the princess began.

'I was rather.'

'Perhaps Raphael . . .'

'Dear boy, we want you to pull a few jobs for us.'

'Oh yes. What did you have in mind? The crown jewels?'

'No, no, of course not. Besides, wouldn't they be rather

difficult to get rid of?' He sniggered a little. 'No, let me begin at the beginning. We have formed ourselves into a society, a pressure group if you like, to bring about certain reforms. Since peaceful pressure over many years has failed we intend to step up our campaign.'

'Make 'em listen,' Miss Cracknell cut it fiercely. It was the first time Jarvis had heard her speak. 'Nobody takes any notice till you rub their noses in it.'

'The major is our strategist,' Raphael went on. 'He has made a study of where and how to apply the pressure.'

'A calculated escalation,' said the major, 'none of this amateur piecemeal picking at it here and there. Hit them so they know each time'll be a bit harder than the time before. That's the strategy. Tactics we leave to you, the chap in the field.'

'Thanks very much.'

'We chose you for your intelligence and planning ability, Mr Chuff,' said the princess.

'I haven't really had a great deal of success or you wouldn't have known where to find me.'

'That was because you were working on your own with limited resources and no cover. All those things we can remedy. No one will connect you with the jobs. It's thought that you've already left the country.'

'I don't want to sound mercenary but what's in it for me?'

'When it's all over, and we've won, a lift out of the country, twenty thousand pounds in a foreign bank plus a block of international stock, enough to give you two thousand a year interest for life. You'll probably want to settle in Tangier or somewhere similar but that of course will be entirely up to you.'

'I'm not a violent man,' Jarvis said, listening to the echo of his own words to Philomela.

'Oh exactly,' said the princess, clasping her pink hands. 'No one must be hurt, you see. That's another reason why we picked you. Planning, Mr Chuff. Your schemes have given me so much pleasure. When I read the account of the last one at your trial I said at once, "That's our man".'

*

He'd always been a keysman. Something he got from his father, Chuff supposed. 'Always fiddling about with little bits of metal as if you didn't have enough of it all day with your pipes and things.' He had inherited his dad's vice and lathe fitted to an old machine treadle like the knifegrinder's. You never knew when the right key would unlock you out of trouble so he always carried a good selection.

With his brown paper carrier and suitcase he'd boarded the train at King's Cross and run up to Edinburgh where he'd booked in at a small hotel, eaten a supper of fish and chips out of the paper, lost himself in the pictures and gone to bed with a noggin from a quarter of Bell's. For a laugh he'd signed the register as George Blake.

In the morning he'd picked a compartment up front, put his suitcase up on the rack, his carrier bag beside him and settled down with the *Daily Express*, a paper pitched between the tabloids and *The Times* which would give him anonymity. He didn't want to be remembered for the cheesecake on his front page or for aspirations to being a Top Person. He needn't have bothered. The handsome charcoal-drawn city slid away with no one else in his compartment. Chuff read on, wincing at the genteel muckraking of the gossip column.

The guard came and clipped his ticket. Chuff rose when he was a carriage ahead and followed him, a passenger in search of morning coffee, a nervous man who took his suitcase with him for fear of being robbed. The guard passed into the mail coach with its bags safely locked in their cage. Jarvis let him go, took out his bunch of keys and locked the compartment behind him, sealing off the rest of the train to reduce the risk of wandering witnesses. Passing through the mail coach he locked the far end and took a poster from his carrier bag which he unfolded and taped quickly to the glass in the door. Returning through the mailcoach he shut himself in the lavatory, opened the suitcase, unpacked the folded mailbag with its prepared labels, put on the guard's cap from the carrier bag and plumped the mailbag with packs of newspaper notes.

The next few moments were the difficult ones. Jarvis adjusted the doorsign to a permanent engaged and peered into the corridor. Nothing moved. He left the lavatory with the door drawn to and held in place by a slip of card and walked firmly to the metal cage, mailbag swung by its neck like a dead goose. Unlocking the cage door he picked out his marked-down bag nestling innocently among the thousands of letters to someone somewhere who was always waiting for one, substituted his own replica, relocked the cage and walked back to the lavatory, expecting at any minute to hear the guard rattling the locked door at the end of the coach or to meet a passenger. The passenger would think nothing immediately of a guard with a mailbag. Only later he would be able to describe Chuff.

Nobody stirred. Chuff ran through the reverse process behind the locked door. Some of the money and the cap went back into the carrier. The rest and the flattened bag filled the expanding suitcase. In five minutes he was strolling through the mailcoach, unlocking the door to the far end and strolling back to let himself through to his own compartment. The poster he left in place. It would be taken for a football fan's glorification of his club. Arsenal for the cup, until they came to put two and two together and wondered why there were no dabs on it.

Back in his compartment he put up the case, took off his gloves and added them to the carrier and hid his trembling and nausea, as reaction set in, behind the *Daily Express* again. He left the train in the first flurry of passengers, melted anonymously into the underground and at Charing Cross took a train for Rye where he booked into a comfortable but inconspicuous hotel. For two days he enjoyed the bitter in the innumerable pubs, wandered the cobbled streets and the surrounding marshes where he sank the suitcase with all his betraying props in a dyke. On the second day he addressed a shoebox full of notes to himself at home from the country and a secondhand book, an enormous boarded Bible whose innards he removed substituting the remaining notes, which he posted at Trafalgar Square. Then he had headed for Thaxsted Road, back from a day by the sea, the perfect tripper. He had even caught the sun a bit. The next day the two parcels had arrived.

'What sort of jobs did you have in mind?'

Raphael wagged a finger. 'That belongs to strategy not

tactics. We shall tell you each one as you go along. Then you'll be able to concentrate just on that. You can ask for anything you want that money can buy. You will think out a plan and . . .'

'Nothing doing. Sometimes you can, sometimes you just have to take pot luck and improvise. You think 'cos you sprung me with a bent screw and an expensive piece of machinery you can do them all like that, whatever they are, but if you're planning a series you need to be flexible and you need them fairly close together for impact. What I say has to go. You can't have a committee sitting on every job.'

Raphael looked uncomfortable. 'Mr Chuff is quite right,' said the princess. 'You must allow for on-the-spot adjustments and a pride in craftsmanship. It's just like the theatre: you never know when you're going to have to ad lib or cover up for a missed cue. Besides Phil will be there.'

Chuff turned to look at her. 'I'm afraid I'm part of the arrangement,' she said.

'I've never worked with anyone before.' He didn't know quite what to say. Having a bird along could be good cover, he could see that, but then again mightn't it louse everything up? Still he had to admit the thought had a lot of attractions.

'Philomela will tell you what each job is. You plan it between you and let us know what you need. But no harm must come to anyone.' Raphael ticked off the points.

'And if we get done?'

'You must try not to, but if you do we'll just have to get you out and away.'

'At each job,' Miss Cracknell was speaking now, gruffly as though she found it hard work or her voicebox was rusted up, 'you'll leave our card with the initials of our society, AHIAR: All Heaven In A Rage.'

'I see,' Chuff considered. 'I can't say I've ever heard of it.'

'No one has yet. But they will soon enough, loud and clear.' The major thumped his stick on the ground like Mr Growser of Children's Hour Toytown.

'And what's it all in aid of?'

'Animals.'

They were all doolally of course, except Philomela. Probably they had some kind of hold over her as they did over him. What they had in mind was very likely something quite harmless and easy. He'd just nodded and said, 'Oh yes.' Then the major had said they must be getting back and they'd all agreed they must be tired. At the top of the stairs he'd said to Philomela, 'I think Philomela's much prettier than Rhoda,' and she'd smiled and wished him good night. Now he lay looking up at the dark, wondering if somehow he'd strayed into Colney Hatch. If he had it was well lined. Could the offer of twenty thousand quid down, with another two grand a year for life, be true? It was no barmier than anything else he'd heard that evening. He didn't fancy Tangier. That was where all the villains made for when they were hot and he liked to be a bit exclusive. He'd think of somewhere: the land of the midnight sun perhaps. 'Oh Aurora Borealis us,' he murmured as he slid towards sleep. 'Animal crackers, that's what they are.'

Waking was to instant recall. He had slept dreamlessly; maybe his brain was convinced it was all a dream and there wasn't room for any other. Although he knew where he was, he lay there peering over the mound of pink sheets at the room like a baby in a pram watching clouds. Light came through the chintzed and leaded window. Outside a bird fluted confidently. Chuff looked at his watch. It was half past eight. By prison hours he had deliciously overslept. Padding to the window he twitched the curtains and looked out. His room was at the back of the house. Beyond was a park still in the undress of late February. Rain fell in small gentle drops. The bird was a black blob, thrush or blackbird size on a high elm branch. Most of Chuff's early nature lore had come from the back of cigarette cards, reinforced by evacuation. If he'd paid attention to Percy Edwards, he thought, he could have told which it was by its song.

Hunger made him hurry through the morning ritual. What

should he do about the bed? He decided to leave it unmade for the moment and look for some breakfast. Not knowing how the day would turn out he had put on the white sweater again over a pair of needlecord levis in a dark moss green. The house outside his bedroom door seemed church quiet. Looking out into the courtyard from the hall windows he saw that the car had gone.

A rustle of papers guided him into the dining room. Philomela was alone at the long table with breakfast things around her, including a half-eaten boiled egg she was neglecting for *The Guardian*.

'Morning,' Jarvis offered uneasily. The paper lowered.

'I hope you slept well.'

'Like a log.' Behind him the body of the night before had bustled in.

'This is Mr Gabriel, Mrs Pinkney. I expect he'd like some breakfast.'

'Tea or coffee?' she demanded.

'Oh tea, please.'

'China or Indian?'

'Indian.'

'And how would you like your egg?'

'Poached, boiled, scrambled or fried?' supplied Philomela.

'Poached,' Jarvis gulped. Mrs Pinkney scurried out. 'I've joined the angels then?'

'Do you mind?'

'As long as no one shortens it to Gabby.'

'Aunt Lottie thought it better.'

'Aunt Lottie?' Philomela didn't answer. 'You mean one of the old ducks last night?' She nodded. 'The princess?' She nodded again. Mrs Pinkney entered with a breakfast tray as if she'd been waiting off for the producer to say 'Now!' Conversation glottal-stopped. It was funny how quickly you learned *not in front of the servants*.

'There now!' said Mrs Pinkney unloading in front of him.

'Lovely,' Jarvis said.

'Is there anything else you'd like?'

'This looks fine, thanks.' Mrs Pinkney was withdrawn. He supposed you couldn't ask the niece of a princess to pour out the tea. Usually when he had a bird stay over for breakfast he got her to preside. Not that he didn't do it day after day for himself but it gave it a more formal touch instead of just sloshing out a mugful as he did every other morning. One of them had made the mistake of calling it gracious living. She hadn't been asked again. He hoped he wouldn't spill it on the polished wood. 'A lovely bit of oak', his mother would have called it, running a loving finger over the surface. 'Solid. None of your new veneered muck.'

'She's not really my aunt,' Philomela was saying. 'Only my father's cousin's wife. But it makes things simpler socially.'

'I'd got you down for a secretary-companion.'

'So I am, in every practical sense.'

'I'm sure you're very practical.'

'As a matter of fact I am.' Chuff nodded, his mouth full of peppered poached eggs and toast. 'In fact I thought when you'd had breakfast we might go over the first job.'

'What do the papers say?'

She passed him *The Times*. 'Much what the television said last night but in more detail. They all agree you're probably basking in the sun by now. I expect you wish you were.'

'Oh here has certain advantages.'

Philomela got up. 'I'll leave you to finish your breakfast in peace. I'll be in the drawing room.' Peace wasn't really something he went much for at that moment, Chuff thought as he poured another cup and mopped up the spilled drops surreptitiously with his shirt, tucking it well down after. He would have to do something about the inner man soon or bust. He couldn't tell if it was a couple of years in stir, Philomela or propinquity that had brought him to such a boil. Leaving the table he felt a nervous urge to fart and ran quickly upstairs so that he could let rip in the safety of the pink bathroom, flacking his arms wildly to disperse the smell of putrescence. 'Jarvis, have you cut the cake? You shouldn't gobble your food so fast.' In the boys' lavatories they had competitions for who could bang one off to order, fastest or loudest. 'There's nothing wrong with your tongue or your farting clapper,' his mother would say when he chattered too much. 'All wind and piss you'll be if you're not careful.' That was how he felt this morning but he'd better go down or she'd wonder what he was up to.

Philomela had a big map of Britain spread on the table. 'That's where we're going,' she pointed.

'Good. Gretna Green.'

'Not quite that far. Ayesguard-on-Edge.' She pointed to a dot in the middle of a large blank piece of Wensleydale.

'What's there? Not much by the look of it.'

'A couple of thousand mink.'

'Coats?'

'You could call them that. They're still on their original owners' backs.'

'You mean running about?' Philomela nodded. 'I thought they all came from Canada.'

'Not these days.'

'And what do we do with them?'

'We let them go.'

'Go where?'

'Wherever they like.'

'But can they live here, I mean, when they're not looked after?'

'As easily as grey squirrels.'

'Which came from America first. I see what you mean.'

'This is a sort of running-in exercise to get us used to working together.'

'Oh I don't think we'd need much practice. I reckon we'd fit rather well.'

'Mr Chuff – '

'Call me Jarvis, even coppers do.'

'If we're going to work together . . .'

'Yes?'

'Do I understand you want to go to bed with me?'

'You could call it that, yes.' For a minute he was shaken. They certainly weren't backward in coming forward, well-educated birds. She'd almost made him blush.

'Well you'll have to wait, possess whatever you call it in patience.'

'Since I've become an angel,' Jarvis said hopefully, 'we could call it my soul, I suppose.'

> A robin redbreast in a cage
> Puts all heaven in a rage.

Each outcry of the hunted hare
A fibre from the brain does tear . . .

Old Morgans scripted carefully across the board and the sixty pens dipped in unison with heads while the hot afternoon droned outside the dusty windows sharpened from time to time with the cries of another class at rounders in the playground. When they had copied it they would learn it and get up to recite, with a team star for the first ten not to stumble.

'A skylark wounded on the wing/A cherubim does cease to sing,' Jarvis recited as they joined the belching, juddering stampede of the M1.

After they had agreed a rough plan Philomela had gone away to get the things they would need leaving him with a very loose end.

'You can go out, into the grounds of course, but it's probably better if you don't go into the village.'

'Do you reckon I should grow a beard?' Chuff asked smoothing his chin. 'I don't go much on fact fungus.'

She regarded him carefully. 'No. Just your hair, I think. Perhaps you could comb it forward into a fringe.'

'Like that?' he fingered it down on to his forehead.

'That's fine.' She was smiling.

'What's funny?'

'Just you. You're such a puritan. It shines out all over you like something out of *Pilgrim's Progress*.' And she had gone leaving him gasping again.

'I think it's "in the wing",' Philomela said now as Jarvis swung out from behind a sugar tanker.

'Anyway that's where it comes from, your society, doesn't it?' He was pleased with his piece of tracking and hoped it would impress her. 'Who's it by?'

'Blake.'

'The one who used to play Adam and Eve in the garden with his wife until the neighbours objected.' He saw her nod out of the corner of his eye. 'I read his life story in the nick. We had to learn the poetry at school.' He had asked if she'd like him to drive and she'd given him the keys.

'It's very American of you,' she said.

'What is?'

'The feeling that you can't let a woman drive you.'

'It's not that. It'd be the same if it was a bloke. I just like driving and when you've been away from it for a couple of years . . .'

'Is your licence valid?' she laughed.

'Lady, it wasn't a dangerous driving charge. As far as I know it's still in order. Not a mark on it.'

Philomela leant back in her seat. 'Actually I'm very lazy and I love being driven.'

'That's all right then. It'll be a bit jumpy at first till I get the feel of it.' Chuff grinned. There didn't seem to be a word he could say that wasn't going in the one direction. But he didn't want to frighten her off. Perhaps he'd better tone it down a bit. There had been silence while he learnt the idiosyncrasies of clutch and gears. 'Like riding a bicycle,' he had been going to say, 'Something you never forget how to do,' but even that had sounded a bit near the knuckle when he tried it out in his head. For something to say he had gone on to the poetry and it had landed him with two naked figures in a garden.

He had gone out into the garden himself after she had left him. The small fine rain had stopped. Down at the bottom of a field rooks were nesting in a clump of tall trees, charred bits of paper flung into the air with a raucous scream as they built their untidy tenements. Chuff had found a path leading away from the house where he could walk without wetting his feet on the hassocks of sodden turf. He guessed the grounds had been laid out at some time to give the best prospect from the windows. The vintage trees were spaced, the ground undulated like a girl. He would be fucking mother nature if he wasn't careful. Turning he looked back at the house. It was calendar perfect. If there'd been snow there'd have been a robin pecking in front of the leaded panes. Low-browed with aged red tiles, steepled with ornate chimneys and fretted with beams, it was the prototype of Everyman's dreamhouse, run up in thousands all over the country in miniature before the war. Some of them were parked semi-detached along the arterial roads; others lay back in their own grounds in select Surrey estates for two-car families. His sense of reality shimmered and distorted like a toothbrush handle seen through a glass of water. He had lost Thaxsted Road perhaps forever. The house looked at him mournfully with eyes glazing with grime, outlined in his imagination across the princess's kitchen. Mice scuttled in the scullery and spiders wove in the backroom like Miss Haversham's wedding breakfast in *Great Expectations*. One day in best John Mills style he might fling back the shredded store curtains and let in the light. But even that was a dream. Madeleine had let it to a nice young couple. He would have to write from Tangier and tell her it was hers to do what she liked with.

From his watch he saw he had been out a long time and was aware of the cold. It was strange how they trusted him to come and go. He could have made off with the spoons if he'd been a fool but that was just it. They knew he was too reasonable. Slowly he walked back to the house and let himself in. It seemed deserted. The dining room had been cleared. He remembered a bookcase in the drawing room which included a row of paperbacks and settled himself by the fire with Maigret. Bird had taught him to pass time.

A gong at one brought him from the grey back streets and shuttered bedrooms of young prostitutes to the dining room. Raphael was already there adjusting his clean napkin across his lap. Mrs Pinkney served them with soup, a cheese pudding and carrots and peas and hot apple pie with cream. Raphael poured red wine from a decanter.

'About St Etheldreda's,' Chuff said when Mrs Pinkney had left them alone.

'Yes, my dear boy?'

'Supposing someone had looked it up and found it was missing?'

'But they didn't, did they? It seems to me exactly the kind of risk you might take yourself. I checked on it of course. If anyone had queried I would have simply pointed out that the parish had been amalgamated with its neighbour after the church was bombed.'

'So you're the vicar of nowhere?'

Raphael looked pained. 'I am the princess's private chaplain. She finds the Established Church not sufficiently attentive to the fall of a sparrow so she has her own private chapel where I officiate. I'll show it to you after luncheon.'

The chapel lay through a shrubbery behind the east wing

where Chuff hadn't explored. Snowdrops dangled their too-heavy heads precariously beside the path. The chapel might have been a dwarf version of the old St Etheldreda's. Raphael pushed open the heavy wooden door and switched on the light. The air inside was thick with damp and incense. Apart from its size it seemed like any other church Chuff had been in, not that there had been many. It had four dark jade green columns, and the altar under its cloth seemed to be of the same material. The paintings on the walls were like those illustrating the school Bibles they had used for scripture lessons.

'Walter Crane,' said Raphael with a sweep of his hand. 'Specially built at the end of the nineteenth century for the great Catholic revival.'

'Oh yes.' A statue of a monk with birds perching all over him like Nelson in Trafalgar Square had a red light burning in front of it and a wolf crouched at the monk's feet. The whole thing seemed crudely cut out of red brick.

'Terracotta by Gil Bones. St Francis of course. The princess commissioned it herself.'

'She must be pretty well heeled?'

'Reasonably so, I believe. There's rather a good small organ that she likes to play and sing to. It's her only outlet now, but it's still a powerful voice. She must have been ravishing as *The Balkan Princess*. I sometimes wonder if that's why she married him, Prince Ferdinand I mean, so that she could play the role in real life. Or it may be that was what attracted him. He had, I believe, a great sense of irony. But that was all before my time.'

But not before his, Chuff thought, seeing his mother's favourite record spinning on the gramophone under the heavy shining round head, its malacca surface worn grey with use and the vocal furred harsh almost beyond recognition. 'You don't get voices like that any more. They broke the mould when they'd made that one,' his mother said while Jarvis wondered about 'they' who made voices and saw a stream of notes pouring into an upturned bell shape for didn't bells have tongues and weren't her top notes 'as clear as a bell'? What other shape could voice moulds be?

'Lottie Shoe,' he said, 'the Portsmouth skylark.'

'My dear boy, you amaze me. And why was she called that? Ah, you don't know. Because her first public appearance was a naval concert at Portsmouth where she wore a sailor suit and sang a sentimental ballad called *Skylark.* You must get her to show you the photos. There's nothing she likes better.'

'If among the angels mother you should see
Ask her if she will come down again
To poor dear father and me,'

they sang around the piano where his father's fingers twinkled and scampered on the black notes putting in the dirt, and aunts and uncles harmonized, taking Kathleen home or lamenting the bird in a gilded cage.

'I always thought it was because of her voice and the way she sort of bubbled out the high notes, if you know what I mean.'

'Coloratura exactly,' said Raphael.

'"Lo hear the genteel la-hark" on Forces' Favourites every Sunday dinner time.'

'What a memory you have, dear boy. It's really quite frightening.' Raphael switched off the light and closed the door. 'We keep it unlocked so that she can slip in any time. Don't be surprised if you hear a ghostly soprano.'

'Mezzo . . .'

'Quite right, mezzo-soprano, from the chapel.'

How would it sound now? As furred and grey as the record maybe. 'You've got yourself a cushy little number here,' Chuff said as they walked back through the shrubbery.

'The princess has been so kind. She raised me when I was fallen, I committed a misdeameanour, a terrible weakness of the flesh which lost me, and justly too, my position of trust. I was sacked from my parish.'

'Choirboys or the poor box?'

'My dear boy, you were right first time.'

'I'm surprised we didn't meet earlier.'

'Oh but we didn't. The disgrace was enough without that.'

'I don't know, you might have rather enjoyed it. Lots of choice and no law to break.'

'I couldn't. All those great rough men.'

'Like me.'

'No, not like you at all. But even you, my dear, with your curiously unsullied air, are too big for me. It has, had I should

67

say, to be something small, and cherubic if you like. You have more the air of a falling angel.'

'Don't tell me,' said Chuff, 'she already has. Gabriel. Did he fall?'

'Only in a rather special sense.' Raphael almost tittered. Chuff had the sensation of having sat down to a card game he didn't know. Everything he said was a card thrown down to see what would follow. There was a kind of running flush to their conversation that had you trying to follow suit, picking up rules as you went along. Almost it might have been a foreign language or Chuff been back kneehigh to a grasshopper with the talk of adults going on over his head where a bright lad might chirp in half-knowingly for the reward of an admiring 'Listen to him'.

As they rounded the corner of the house a glossy horse lifted its head from mumbled attention of rubber lips to a patch of lawn. 'Althea's come,' said Raphael and quickened his pace. The horse blew at them disdainfully. Through the windows Jarvis saw the second old duck from last night in riding kit, stamping in the hall.

'Lottie not here?'

'She and Philomela have gone up to town.'

'Thought I'd ride over. Couldn't stand the waiting about. Alex is such a stick with his strategy. He can sit all day playing patience. When's the first job?'

'We're leaving tomorrow,' Chuff answered. 'Then when we've spied out the land a bit we'll move in as soon as we can. I can't really say more than that.'

'No, no. Course you can't. I see that.' Miss Cracknell nodded. If she'd had a riding crop, Jarvis thought, she'd have slapped it against her boot. 'When you get back get Philly to bring you over. Show you the stables. Remind me of a lad I had once. No offence. Had the best seat ever and gentle as a girl if girls ever were gentle. Some of them ride as if they weren't on flesh and blood. Still mustn't get started on that. Tell Lottie I called, and don't forget . . .' She turned back to Chuff, 'get Philly to bring you over. Never could get that girl to ride. Know she'd have been good.'

Silently Jarvis agreed and hoped he'd have more luck. Then Miss Cracknell was gone, swinging up into the saddle like Buck Jones and wheeling off through the park, her small upright figure on the big horse shrinking into a silhouette between two tall trees that put up the rooks in an indignant clamour.

'A spot of shuteye for me,' said Chuff. 'Got to get me strength up.' The wine and the unreality were making him drowsy. Someone else could sit in for him for a while. He climbed the shallows stairs to his pink room, undressed to his pants and socks and crept under the covers. 'Must learn to ride filly,' he thought as he fell asleep.

Well at least he was driving her. When he had woken it had been to a room full of soft dusk. He had had a bath and dressed in one of the suits in the belief that a change was as good as a rest and that a purposeful tailored Chuff might catch her eye. At the top of the stairs he shot two elegant frills of pale pink cuff fit for a Mississippi gambler. Tonight he would be the cocksure Rhett. He wished he was dark. He had hung his Ashley pale other self in the wardrobe when he took out the suit but there was nothing to be done with his thatch of insipid hair. It was all very well for Greek gods and Nazi stormtroopers but tonight he wanted to be a gentlemanly pirate and they were always raven-haired and blackavised.

Again he was deflated while he stood knocking on the door as if he had been sent to the off licence and waited peering through the opening into the bar beyond at the smoke and voices. Good manners precluded his making an entry and reduced him to sidling in when he was called. The scene was set like the evening before except that the galloping major and his sister were absent. Tonight he was invited to help himself to a drink. They watched the news again but there was nothing further on him and if there had been Chuff wouldn't have believed it. He no longer seemed the person who had lived that strange grey pond life for nearly two years.

Through dinner the princess chatted with Chuff and Raphael. 'Now I have two guardian angels,' with a pat for each. Philomela said little. After coffee the princess said she was tired and that a little meditation and then bed after the rush of the city, if Chuff would excuse her, would be best. Raphael followed her out.

'Did you get everything?' Chuff asked when they'd gone.

'Yes. I invented a nephew on an outward bound course.'

Chuff thought he caught a distant sound of music. 'They've gone to the chapel?'

'Aunt Lottie finds it relaxing to belt out a selection from the English Hymnal before bed.'

'And what do you find relaxing?'

'To read in the bath. I'm rather tired too.'

'I'm sorry I couldn't come with you.'

'It's not your fault. You'll have plenty to do for the next few days. But London is probably the one place where you shouldn't be seen.' She yawned. 'I'm sorry but I think I must go to bed. Help yourself to anything you want. I'll see you in the morning.'

He was left to his glass and more Maigret. Help yourself to anything you want. That was just what he couldn't do, couldn't even undress her in his head, not knowing how she would strip, how it might be. He went to kick the logs in the fireplace making them flare and spit like a cat. For a few minutes he tried to think about tomorrow, to run through their rough plan and visualize how it would go. That wouldn't come either. It was a speculative blank like Philomela's body. His only anchorage was the far past while the most recent was as distasteful and vacant as a girl you'd once had, all open pores and yoghourt sour breath once the bloom was off. Mulling his glass of whisky first against the flames and then in his hot mouth he let it trickle in little spirts down his throat. What had she said that morning? At least it hadn't been no, not for ever.

Next day they had loaded up the Rover after breakfast. The princess and Raphael had come to the front door to wave them off as if they were going on a honeymoon. Chuff had taken the keys and driven them through a sunlit countryside, bypassing Oxford, until they were snorting north with what seemed like half London.

'Doesn't everyone?' she asked.

'What?'

'Learn that piece at school. I know I did.'

'I suppose so but most people forget it. I had until now.'

'That's our conditioning. If we all remembered, it would make life too difficult.'

'How did you get into this?'

'You mean here, now? This car with you?'

'If you like.'

'It's hard to explain. Part of it is my fondness for them all. They were so determined that I was afraid they would get themselves into terrible trouble so I took a hand to prevent it, if possible.'

'I don't see how your helping them will stop it.'

'They were going to go it alone, you know, the spirit of Dunkirk and all that.'

Chuff had to laugh at the idea of the major leading a cavalry charge up Whitehall of centenarians on carthorses or in wheelchairs. 'What are they after?'

'An international charter for animals to end all exploitation of one species by another.'

'They're barmy.'

'Maybe,' Philomela sighed, 'but they're also deadly serious, as serious as any other minority group that feels it has a neglected cause. They feel they've been reasonable and patient too long while things have got steadily worse. They're all old, soon they'll be dead and that makes them a bit reckless.'

'And what do you think?'

'What I think doesn't come into it.'

'Whose idea was it to spring me then?' Chuff asked, hoping that it had been hers.

'The major came up with the idea of someone. He said it had been done in the war, that special units had been made of convicts or men released from prison if they had special skills that would be of use to the commandos or Resistance forces.'

'Petermen used to jellying safes could be put on to blowing up railways and things. I see that.'

'Aunt Lottie picked you.'

'That was nice of her.'

'You sound as if you mind.'

'Mind! I was bleeding wild at first I can tell you.'

'I should have thought . . .'

'Anyone'd be only too pleased to get out of the nick. Well, thank you very much, lady, for the kind thought, but as a matter of fact we don't want your handouts, we prefer to manage our own lives even if it means starving to death.' Chuff jammed his foot on the accelerator and the car rocketed up the outside lane at a smooth ton.

'The limit's seventy,' said Philomela. 'We don't want to be picked up.'

'Speak for yourself.' Chuff knew he was being childish. He eased a little on the pedal. 'Maybe nothing would suit me better than to get back to a nice quiet bit of bird.'

'Then why did you agree to be sprung?' Philomela's calm and rational articulation drove the pedal down again.

'Because Father flaming Raphael blackmailed me.'

'But he wouldn't have carried it out.'

'How the hell was I to know that? I didn't know he was part of a madhouse. He might have been for real.'

'This is for real.'

'It might seem real to you, lady, but to me it's a kids' tea party in the bin.'

'I'm sorry, I just don't see why you're so angry. If you like you can get out at the next town and give yourself up.'

'You don't understand, do you? That's your whole trouble, people like you. You've interfered in my life and already I'm not the same person. Now you say calmly, "Go back." Just on an elementary level I've lost me remission. Your interference has cost me a third longer inside, let alone the constant harrying and watching I'd get.' As he tried to explain, the needle on the speedometer sank to seventy.

'Is that really what you're angry about?'

'That's just some of it.' Even to himself he couldn't have explained what the rest was.

'All right,' said Philomela calmly, 'when we've done this job you can take me to bed. Now perhaps you'll concentrate on the driving or let me.'

The speedometer zoomed past eighty, then settled back to a controlled sixty-nine point five.

They had left the main road for sandwiches and beer. 'The first pint for nearly two years,' Jarvis smacked holding the liquid amber up to the light to admire it properly. 'I remember this brew from my training days at Catterick. We can't be far away.'

'Did you like the army?'

'Not a minute of it. It was all bullshit or getting shot at. If I'd known enough about it I'd have been a conchie but they catch you when you're still wet behind the ears before you've had time to think that there might be a way out. At least they used to. The kids are more fly these days. I like to think conscription wouldn't work any more.'

'What about the regular army?'

'You always get some people who are basically violent. Putting them in the army or the cops siphons it off legally.'

'Do you believe that?'

'Yes,' Chuff said carefully, 'I do. Unless they're not thinking when they join, they must agree that by putting on the uniform they're prepared to shoot at someone or be shot at. In the police you must expect to use force or have it used against you. There are a few of them who feel they're doing a social service but if that's what they want they would be probation officers. Being a copper is only the other side of the coin from being a villain, like looking in the mirror.'

'Then you should feel a lot in common with them.'

'No,' said Chuff, 'because I'm not that kind of villain.'

'Are there different kinds?'

'When I said a mirror I meant full length. The mobsters at the top, like the Krays for instance, they're the equivalent of the top brass fuzz with their gangs and plans, organized crime as they call it. They're the ones who run the vice rings and porn shops, casinos, protection rackets, all that and they've got a working relationship with their opposite numbers, blue films for cops' parties, plenty of dropsie and girls when needed, holidays abroad and so on. Then there's the vice squad who ponce around soliciting for someone to pick them up so they can hang a charge on them.'

'I thought they were forbidden to solicit.'

'What else is it if you stand about looking lonely and come hitherish in places where that sort of lurking is for that sort of trade? Doesn't matter if it's men or women. The copper and his mark are like two players on opposite teams in football sticking like grim death to each other to make sure neither of them gets away with anything. Then on the bottom deck there's the thickies in their big boots busy with all the day-to-day petty jobs, half-inching and tea-leafing, that go on all the time.'

'If there weren't any villains there wouldn't be any fuzz.'

'Then what would you do with the kind of person who makes a good cop? They'd be unemployable. There's nothing else suited to their talents. Think of their usual insolence when they speak to you. Where else would they get away with that? And I don't mean with hard cases like me. I mean with just anyone they happen to speak to in the street.'

'They're different on the continent. Much politer. They salute and call you the equivalent of sir or madam.'

'Whereas here it's usually "squire".'

'What kind of villain are you?' Philomela asked as they followed the signposts to Ayesguard-on-Edge deeper into the moors.

'Maybe you'll find out in time.' Chuff looked through the window at the scurrying tweed of turf flecked here and there with sheep like mossy white boulders. The road snaked over shoulders and through gullies climbing all the time. 'Christ, it's bleak. Must be terrible up here in the winter.'

'Urban man Chuff, that's you.'

'You don't mean to say you like it.'

'Out of a warm car window it's got a certain wild something.'

'So have I in a warm bed.'

'Turn left here; it'll bring us out above the farm.'

They lay in a wash of pale spring sunshine looking down at the valley below while the wind tugged at their clothes and the stiff grass. The Rover was out of sight under the hill, run off the track into a natural lay-by behind an outcrop of tall rocks stained with the heavy weep of winter.

'That's it,' said Philomela passing Chuff the glasses. A handsome stone farmhouse stared up the valley. Behind stretched a garden, now windbitten and leafless. Next came a small orchard and then a fenced paddock with rows of cages. To the side were outbuildings. A small stream dashed itself down the hillside. Somewhere behind them a lark flung into the air and began to burble its way up the ladder of sky.

'Looks like a miniature nick,' Chuff said, 'with those cages and that fence.'

'Then it's death row.'

Jarvis adjusted the high-powered sights and took a bead on one of the cages. The animal inside seemed to be sunning itself. 'Pretty little devil. Like an otter or a big weasel. Looks blue in this light.'

'Some of them are. We're just in time. In a couple of weeks it'll be the mating season and then everyone'll be much more alert.'

'Including the mink.' Chuff examined the wire compound. 'We'll have to cut through the fence, a hole big enough for us to get in and them to get out. There's bound to be a dog in that farm. Each cage is fastened with a bolt. It'll take some time to let that lot out.'

'You see those two huts.'

'What about them?'

'They've probably got more animals in them on an open plan basis.'

'Right. We'll hit one of those first, the one furthest from the car, so that if they're on to us by then it's not so far to run. I'll cut that phone just as a precaution. Can you see anyway up to the farm apart from that drive?'

'No.'

'Then we'll wire up the gate so they can't get after us. Now let's get back to the car. This wind's death to brass monkeys.'

'Supposing they won't come out of their cages?' Jarvis said when they were back in the comfort of the Rover.

'From all I've read I think they will. Mink are curious like most animals and they're nocturnal. That means they'll be pretty lively at night.'

'There's only one thing going for us as far as I can see and that's absolute silence. At least the cages should open easily. We won't attempt it until one o'clock.'

Philomela lit a cigarette and blew a long provocative cloud of smoke at the window. Jarvis cleared his throat. Sitting so close in the car was a kind of torture. 'I suppose you wouldn't consider anticipating a bit?'

'After the job.'

Chuff sighed. 'Must be the mating season. What will happen to them once they're away?'

'Some of them will be trapped or shot or hunted by hounds. Some will go wild and survive. Which would you rather do? Stay in a comfortable prison and be painlessly put down at the end of the year or take your chance under those conditions?'

'Oh I'd take me chance every time if it was that or a certain chop. How do they do it?'

'Painless injection. It's called "pelting". Officially once they're loose they're pests. Look.' She took a leaflet out of the glove compartment. Chuff read through it.

'Public enemy number one. They've even got him mugged and printed.' The mink surprised in a clump of grass and reeds snarled at the camera. Its spoor marched across the back page.

'Some people would argue that since they're not natives here and have been bred in captivity . . .'

'I know, they've never known any different. That's the next one to coals-in-the-bath when it's humans.' Chuff felt himself warming to the mink. 'I wouldn't mind being so beautiful you'd want to wear me.'

'Even if you had to die for it?'

They had eaten more sandwiches and drunk coffee from a Thermos put up by Mrs Pinkney. Then Philomela had got on to the back seat and curled up like a cat to sleep the afternoon away while Jarvis had dozed in front. Nothing passed on the track. Occasionally a sheep lifted its head to peer at them but soon they took no notice and munched on at the unappetizing-looking scrub.

The worst of the waiting was still to come when they woke again. Sky and sun had turned to a huge white oyster shell with one milky pearl low down on its rim. Philomela stretched and shivered.

'There's a long time to go yet,' said Chuff.

She sat up. 'I'm going for a short walk,' she said, 'alone,' and opened the back door. Chuff watched her stride off among the rocks and prickly gorse. It was a good walk, poised without mincing. With her she seemed to take what was left of the day's colour, draining it away into her receding figure so that the white sky became desolate and he wanted to call out to her to come back soon. He knew then how it would be to see her off at a station or airport. To pass the time he got out the remainder of the food and drink, including the replenished flask from the glove compartment. They would need something against the damp cold that began to seep up from the turf as the sun paled and sank. Soon too it would be dark and unwise to draw attention to themselves with lights.

Chuff was used to waiting. They had taught him that in the army and he had kept himself in training. But Philomela chafed like a horse held too long under starter's orders, lighting one cigarette after the other which glowed in the dark car, suffusing her face like an angry firefly as she drew on the smoke. Conversation flourished and died in taut spasms. Later she slept again. They were both too conscious of their unresolved closeness to draw together for warmth. Chuff took his turn among the gorse bushes.

At eleven thirty they climbed the slope to look down on the farm. Only one light showed. The hills fell away round them, black on grey in the starlight. They crept under the lee of the hill and watched for the light to be doused. Suddenly Chuff heard a noise like clattering shale.

'Must have been a sheep,' he whispered.

'Silly, it's my teeth. Can't help it. Reflex action. The cold.'

He wanted both to laugh and put his arms round her. 'Go back to the car. I'll watch.'

'N-n-no!' she chattered obstinately. A door opened below. A dog ran barking into the garden; then was silent. Chuff could visualize the cocked leg. Then it began to bark again, frantically. Whistles and cries called it in but it was some time before the dog obeyed. A sound of a door shutting in the clear air released a sigh from Chuff.

'That's all right. The dog's one of those daft ones that barks at anything. So if it barks at us they won't take any notice.'

The light went out downstairs. 'Must be one in a bedroom round the back,' Chuff said. 'We'll go back to the car, get ready and move at a quarter to one.'

The first job was to camouflage the car. A moon was rising

and its radiance highlit the Rover in every detail. Chuff took a black polythene car cover from the boot, cut doors and windows in it with a hardbacked razor blade and taped it into position so that the car could be driven with its mask on. From their vantage on the hill they had been able to see other vehicles far off by their headlights but nothing had come this way and the track that led towards the farm itself was a private road. The road they were on now led past the back of the farm, with an embankment running down towards the wire fence. Their return to the car would be uphill but there was nothing to be done about that.

At a quarter to one Chuff started the engine and climbed the car back on to the road. Once on the gradient he cut the engine and let them coast silently down till they were under a clump of bushes that shielded the road from the farm. Leaving the doors ajar they got out of the shrouded car and slid down the bank to the fence. Black stockings darkened and disguised their faces. They wore uniform black sweaters and jeans.

While Philomela crouched beside the fence Chuff crept away to wire the farm gate and cut the telephone wire.

'Supposing there were an emergency and they had to call the doctor or the fire brigade?' Philomela had queried.

'He'd have to fetch them by car. You can't have it all ways.'

Chuff slithered on the damp turf, feeling eyes on him from every blank window of the house, but the first part went easy. The telephone wire gave with a small ping and he was soon crouched behind the gate lashing it tightly to its post with wire. He had taught himself to be as deft in gloves as out of them. He doubled back towards Philomela and set to work on the wire fence, nipping out a piece of mesh and bending it back so that there was a section wide enough for them to creep through. In the moonlight he ducked his head at Philomela and her anonymous figure nodded back at him. They might have been two ghoulish dummies in their uniforms or cut-outs from the blacker cloth of the night sky. Chuff led the way through the gap. They were in.

Soft-footed they moved towards the far barn, conscious of the flickering movements of caged animals all around them. Chuff wrinkled his nose under the mask. Mink stinks. They were certainly nocturnal little beasts. Eyes gig-lamped at them as they passed. Paws clung to the mesh lifting the furry bodies to press curiously towards them. Noses whiffled questioningly.

The barn door was barred and padlocked. Chuff drew out his keys. The lock was a simple cheap affair and gave no trouble. Philomela lifted the bar out of its socket. Holding their breath they drew the door gently open. Philomela led the way in and flicked on a pencil of torchlight. A wire fence ran from end to end of the barn with another padlock holding a meshed door. Beyond the door the floor seethed with soft blue fire wherever the torchbeam fell. It was coated with living sapphire fur that heaved and flowed like water or wind-moved grass. Here and there a snout lifted and eyes looked up greenly at the beam. The reek of animal musk and feeding stuff in which cod-liver oil seemed to play a strong role was almost overpowering. Chuff undid the padlock and opened the gate. There was a moment's pause. A bolder creature sat up on its back legs otter-style, its nose working furiously, perhaps scenting the draught of freedom from the door. Dropping to all fours, it ran forward with one or two others hesitant behind. Again it paused while Philomela and Chuff watched fascinated. Then, with a sudden belt, it was through the wire fence, passing them and out into the night.

As if a dam had broken the others poured after it in a blue stream that flowed round their ankles as they stood there. Chuff felt a sharp nip. Someone had taken a bite in passing. Ungrateful little bugger. Philomela slid a card between the wire meshes and followed him into the yard. If the still-caged animals had been restless before they squirmed with life now. Hundreds of feet drummed softly on the wire netting as they ran up and down their cells. It was a noise that reminded Chuff of the fits of banging that overtook the nick at moments of communal despair, anger or delight. He had heard it during his first stretch before the ending of the death penalty when a moronic farm labourer was being topped for strangling a girl. The cons had beaten on their pipes with mugs, spoons, anything that would make row enough to hammer on those doors. No one knew if the man inside heard. No one ever came back to tell you. Now the mink were drumming.

Swiftly they set about opening the cages, hampered by the

need for quiet. The animals helped, curving out of the half-raised flaps like scimitars of glistening velvet in the moonlight. Chuff hoped they were finding the gap. On and on they went down the rows till he was dizzy with repetition. From time to time he looked up at the house astounded that no light had gone on as a flap seemed to scream of metal on metal in the night or one of the mink hit the ground with a thud. As he passed the usual gate he saw that many of them were bunched beside it. He undid the padlock and let them flow out into the night to vanish in the paddock.

At last there was only the second barn. This time they knew the drill. Inside the torch lit up a river of cream. When it was safely pouring follow-my-leader into the dark Chuff and Philomela stepped into the enclosure. It was then that the light went on in the house and the dog began to bark excitedly. Chuff darted back to the paddock gate and closed it; snapping the padlock to and nipping it hard to jam the mechanism. Philomela was already throught the wire and clambering up the bank. Jarvis ducked to waist level and ran behind a row of cages to scramble through the hole. He heard a window flung up and froze in deep shadow at the bottom of the embankment. Philomela had already made the safety of the bushes.

Turning his head Chuff saw a figure silhouetted at the lit window. 'Christ,' he thought, 'he's got a gun.' Now another figure appeared beside it. With half a bit of luck nothing would be obvious from the window. The figures were snatched away. Jarvis took a breath and ran up the bank, round the bush and into the passenger seat, ripping off his mask. Philomela fired the engine and they ran forward lightless down the track.

'Right here,' he said. Philomela swung the car up an even steeper gradient that led over the hill and down into a hollow. She pulled up leaving the engine running. They leapt out, stripped the car of its covering, themselves of their uniform sweaters, bundling them into the boot. Jarvis took the wheel, respectable in fur hat and coat, while Philomela wriggled out of her jeans and into a dress on the back seat. With half his mind on the tantalizing glimpses he could see in the mirror, he drove by moonlight towards a main road.

'Ready?' he asked, but he could see that she was composed now, her shoulder-length hair neatly combed, as if from an evening out. He switched on the lights and, picking up the main road, gunned the motor towards the south-west.

For a while they were silent, feeling the exhaustion that follows a supercharge of adrenalin. Then the need for confirmation and reassurance pressured them into speech.

'Do you think he found out?' Chuff asked over his shoulder, 'or just went back to bed?'

'I couldn't be sure. No one came out while you were climbing up the bank but the bedroom light was still on. I could hardly see you and I knew where to look but they must have heard the engine start unless the dog was making too much noise and the walls muffled the sound.'

'Anyway the sooner we can get lost in civilization the better. How are we doing?'

'Pull up a minute and let me come in front. I'm useless back here and I can't hear what you're saying.'

'Do you think they all got away?' Chuff asked when they were going again.

'I hope so but they'll probably recapture a few.'

'They certainly come in all colours, your furry friends. That last lot was like Siamese cats. Maybe we should have swiped one for a pet. When I was a kid there was a boy whose father kept ferrets. He brought one to school one day inside his shirt. Some blokes put them down their trousers for a bet but I reckon that's a bit dodgy and a bit kinky too. But I always remember this kid with a little wicked furry head poking out between his shirt buttons. You'd have to housetrain it and bath it so it didn't pong so much.'

'That's the musk glands.'

'Like a skunk? But they wouldn't stink so if they hadn't all been bodged up together. Like nicks, they smell, sour of a lot of blokes together with no one to get done up for. After a bit your nose doesn't notice but when you first go in it hits you like stale breath.'

'They'll ravage the countryside of course. They like chicken and pheasant and fish.'

'So do humans. They're not daft, your mink.'

'Why mine?'

'I dunno. They reminded me of you somehow: beautiful and very well-bred. Aristocrats.'

She laughed for the first time since they had set out that morning. 'What do you know about my breeding?'

'I don't have to. Even if your mother was a street-walker and your father a bookie you're still class. You can't help it. What my mother used to call "one of nature's gentlemen", if you'll forgive the unisex. Like mink, although I suppose you could say they're only a kind of classy rat.'

'They haven't got very gentle natures.'

'I'll say. One of the little sods took a swipe at my ankles as he was on the way out. What was on the visiting cards?'

'Just: *All Heaven In A Rage.*'

'Printed?'

'Not professionally.'

Chuff cleared his throat. 'Can I say you were bloody good without getting me face slapped?'

'I wasn't too much of a drag?'

'Bloody marvellous.'

'It must be hard when you're used to working alone.'

'Adaptable, that's me. Go anywhere, do anyone.' Jarvis laughed. Suddenly he was happy as a sandboy, whatever that might have been. Jarvis had always seen him digging alone on the shore, with bucket and spade and a great sandcastle whose towers were perfect pail-shapes and whose walls never crumbled as the wind dried and grained them while the wavelets unfurled gently as golden syrup and the boy laughed and sang out to sea. 'What's a sandboy, Mum?'

'I dunno, dear. Maybe a boy who went round selling sand like the gippos with their heather and clothes pegs and the lavender woman. "White sand and grey sand, who'll buy my grey sand?"' But in his mind's eye the sand was yellow and darkened with sea. 'I'm the king of the castle and you're the dirty rascal.' Bandychaired between his parents after a long day out or given a flying angel on his father's shoulders he had been prince of the sandcastle until he had been old enough to realize he was only a dirty rascal like the rest.

'Shall I drive for a bit? You must be tired.'

'So must you.'

'I didn't do as much as you and you drove all the way up as well.'

'I'm afraid I might fall asleep if I gave up now.'

'Would that matter?'

'No,' Chuff said, surprised. 'I suppose it wouldn't,' and drew in to the side of the road.

When he woke it was because the car had stopped again. His tongue and mouth were rank and furred. 'What's up?'

'I have to take a walk.'

'After you.'

There was a mouthful of cold coffee that they shared. 'I'll take over for a bit,' said Chuff. 'Where are we and what's the time?'

Philomela drew deeply on a cigarette. 'We're nearly at Kendal and it's five past four.'

'The sun gets up at about half past six.' Beyond the warmth of the car the cold blackness stretched like an underground lake without bottom. It was the lowest hour of morning when humans shrank to trollsize as they tunnelled towards the dawn. 'At Kendal we turn left. I'll take it easy. It'd be better if we weren't noticed till a more respectable time.' Even so they were forced to run off the road and pass an hour under some trees while the car turned to a cold metal coffin around them without the heater. As the sky began to stripe grey behind bannering sunrise, Chuff switched on again and they trundled down the last half hour into Kendal where a lorry-drivers' steamy warm pull-in was serving breakfast they were almost too tired to eat. Philomela went away to wash and brush up while Jarvis drank another cup of tea. Then they drove south for a few miles among a shoal of early lorries till they found a branch road leading towards the sea.

'Morecambe Bay, Gracie Fields's country. Surely there'll be a motel open along here.'

'It's early in the season,' Philomela doubted but Jarvis's faith was rewarded by a cluster of Swiss chalets under a neon arrow.

'If you'll just sign the book,' the receptionist said.

Philomela took the pen. Out of the corner of his eye Jarvis saw she had written: M. and A. Gabriel.

'Number thirteen, Mr Gabriel, if you're not supersitious.'

'Not a bit.'

They parked the car outside the varnished pitch pine façade. 'Look,' said Chuff pointing to the chalet name painted on a slice of treetrunk, 'Mont Blanc. I hope that doesn't mean the beds.'

'As long as they're there. And anyway it might have been William Tell or Cuckoo Clock and we wouldn't have got a bit of sleep. I'm so tired I feel as if I'm dying.'

Chuff carried through the cases. Suddenly he felt shy as if it was his first time again. But he needn't have bothered. Philomela had stripped to her underwear in a flash, whisked into the bathroom and out and was under the nearest blankets while he was still wondering. 'You were bloody good too, Chuff,' she muttered drowsily. Jarvis smiled, draped his clothes methodically and slid into the other single. He could have, he knew he could have, but it was better to wait. Groaning he realized they had forgotten to hang out the *Do Not Disturb* notice and hauled himself out of bed again to the door. Philomela didn't move. From the depth of her breathing he guessed she was already asleep. Suddenly he felt a terrible weak tenderness envelop him as if he was going to pipe his eye. Scrambling into bed he buried his hot face in the cool welcome of a pillow.

His watch when he surfaced told him they had slept till dinnertime but he still didn't feel hungry. As quietly as he could he had a long bath, lying back so that his legs floated. Meticulously he soaped and lathered his genitals, drawing back the foreskin to make sure the head was absolutely clean and frothing the soap down the crease between his buttocks where the waxy sweat gathered. Twice he shampooed the fuzz of short hairs, letting the water rinse among the standing curls like floating pondweed. His armpits came in for their share. He had never been so clean since it'd been his mother's job to bath him.

She had promised and she wasn't the kind of cockteaser to

go back on it but he wanted her to want him, not be put off by some goaty old whiff at the crucial moment. Chuff shaved and brushed his teeth twice. By the time he emerged from the bathroom he was newborn and tingling like a toothpaste commercial. Most of our lives, he thought, are spent sleeping, excreting and grooming like other apes just to enjoy the bits in between.

Philomela looked at him out of half an eye. 'You're up,' she said thoughtlessly.

'How do you like a life of crime?'

'Crime,' she said, suddenly throwing back the clothes, 'is a relative thing like living in sin.'

Chuff watched with pleasure as she bent over her suitcase. 'Let's go to the seaside,' she said, pulling out assorted clothes and heading for the bathroom. Left alone Chuff cased the room thoroughly, running to earth what he privately christened a 'gobbling teasemaid'. By her return he had two cups of hot instant coffee. He milked the small cardboard udder into one of them.

'I'm glad to see you're house-trained.'

'Comes of living by yourself.'

Philomela took hers black with sugar. Silence strained between them. 'Shall we go?' she said, draining the cup quickly. Outside yesterday's thin disc of sun was shining again. 'Oh I do like to be beside the seaside,' turned a fairground roundabout in Chuff's head.

The day was a slow build-up to pleasure in which he made love to her through long hours, becoming sunlight so he could finger her face and salt to lie on her lips and be taken in by her tongue. He made his wanting the air she breathed so that it would be all around her and inside her. Like a thief he lulled and watched until he knew her every movement before he crept in to take and take. How would it be: robbery with violence, a blag? At times during the day he wanted to force her at once. Or a simple hoist, in and out without complaint, easy as taking candy from a baby.

It was late afternoon when they got back, yawning with fresh air and the sleepless night before. Jarvis unlocked the door and followed her into Mont Blanc. She took off her coat and began to hang it up in the white painted cupboard. Her back was to him, vulnerable and inviting. He stepped up behind her and put his arms round her, pulling her buttocks against him. For a moment she smoothed the hanging coat as if he wasn't there. Then she put her hands on his as they moved up to her breasts and pressed them down hard.

Quietly she said, 'You might not like me.'

'I just fucking want you. I can't hold it any longer.' He turned her round to kiss her and as he felt her respond and her arms go round his neck, he reached behind for the long zip and ripped it down, digging his nails into the bared flesh of her back and beginning to peel the dress from her shoulders so that he could bite gentle at her throat and the succulent curves of breast above the top of her slip. She smelt warm and musky.

'Take your clothes off,' she said and turned away from him. Without difficulty or hesitation she pared away all her clothing, it seemed in one movement except for the initial kicking off of shoes. His mouth dry, Chuff tried to match her economy but by the time he was naked she had slipped under the bedclothes.

'Fetch me an ashtray.'

Chuff padded obediently to the table, away of being watched. She was lying back against the pillows, her heavy breasts on the folded top sheet showing the delicate pink nipples just as he liked them. He never cared for gobstoppers or chapel hatpegs. 'Yes,' she said, 'I like you. Are you coming into this bed?'

Three

'Nature only brought us into the world to love.'

'What did you do in the Great War, Daddy?' asked Chuff as they drove south in the morning.

'How do you mean?'

'Before this little caper?'

'I've done lots of things. My last was personal assistant to a film producer/director making a film about gambling in Monaco.'

'Did it ever get shown?'

'Not much over here except in places like the Paris-Pullman. It was in French.'

'You speak French?'

'Yes. I went to school in France for a while.'

'Being finished off?' Philomela nodded. 'They made a bloody good job of it I'll say that for them.'

'I think anything useful I know I taught myself after I left. I had to.'

'I don't suppose you'd have starved if you hadn't. Your Aunt Lottie would have looked after you.'

'Yes, but you can't go on spongeing on people just because they're related to you, and even that's a bit distant.'

'I thought that was how your lot did it: nepotism.'

'She's very sweet but I would never have learnt anything useful under Aunt Lottie's wing.'

'She must have known all about it once. Lottie Shoe had hundreds of admirers, stagedoor Johnnies with their arms full of orchids and bubbly.'

'I don't think any of that would be much use now,' Philomela smiled.

'I don't know, I'd come round your door any day,' with a flagging daffodil and a pint of Guinness, Chuff thought bitterly. They brought you up on legends of beauty and what was its due and then told you none of it was for you.

'Why did you do it?' Philomela broke into his thoughts.

'Do what? Get caught? Because I couldn't help it.'

'No. All of it.'

'That's what they all want to know. I'd have thought it was obvious.' From the first time he had been nabbed at nine the same questions had been thrown at him. That had been kid's stuff: all of them in the gang filching and scrumping by turns and turnabout. It'd been his go to get the batteries from the bike shop for the torches someone else had whipped. Temptingly they stood in neat rows on the counter. While Swede and Knocker had ostentatiously admired the bikes standing proudly in their chocks, gleaming black as Hopalong Cassidy's horse in their utility strip, keeping the assistants distracted, Chuff had palmed two Ever Ready's into his pocket and was reaching for two more when the hand fell on his shoulder. Swede and Knocker had panicked, landing the lot of them in the bag. It was his first known offence and he had got off with probation but now they were a notorious gang, equals of Leo Gorcey and the Bowery Boys. Swede was the dopey one, the Huntz Hall, and the only one who wasn't a vaccy. Somehow Chuff had to fight off the shame of his parents coming down from London for the trial. His Dad had spoken well but quietly so that the chairman had asked him to speak up and their voices had sounded both familiar and foreign among the country burrs and the upper-class dialect of the officials so that he was proud and ashamed together. Then the chairman had ticked them all off about ruining the war effort and warned them that next time they'd be put away.

'I hear any more tales about you,' said his mother, 'I'll come down and give you such a damn good clout you'll wake up in the middle of next week with some sense knocked into you.' Later he realized she was frightened for him. Whenever she could she sent him five-shilling postal orders and those letters exhorting him to be good. Old Morgans had driven them hard in their last year. Chuff had been just out of probation when he set off in his new harsh grey flannel uniform for his first morning at the high school.

While he was still a junior tadpole the strange new life had kept him busy. By twelve he was a tall thin boy, whitefaced and fair-haired, a young storm trooper guiltily *siegheiling* himself in the glass although the war effort wasn't needed any more so no one could accuse him of sabotage. Except himself. Madeleine's attempts to become a GI bride had all failed. She had taken a Pitman's course and joined the white-collar girls catching the underground to the Bank every morning and lamenting over nylons snagged on the wooden seats. In the evening she sat with a minute crochet hook picking up ladders rung by rung while her face set like a clown's under its yeastpack. Hours were spent poised on the fender in front of the mirror over the fireplace while she squeezed at blackheads and plucked her eyebrows into innocent surprise.

Chuff didn't know whether his sister or Crawler Edwards amazed and angered him more. It was worse in a way to have it in the family but then again Crawler didn't even have the thin disguise of sex over his carryings-on. He was always tidy, punctual and first with his hand up. And it wasn't because he liked what they were doing, Jarvis was sure of that. Scalpel Sherman for instance had decided he was going to be a doctor and that was fair enough. He was always putting in extra time in the labs, reading books with mapped out bodies in them other than the reproductory system, but although he was ragged he was respected or at least his barmy passion was. Yet with Crawler it was different, not what he wanted to do but what he wanted to be.

'And it'd behove you to be more like him,' his mother had said when he had complained one day. 'You could be anything from where you are. No need to be pig-ignorant like me all your life.'

'You're not,' he said fiercely, 'you know lots of things.'

'Like what? Your father knew things. You'd do better to take after him.'

'But he never got anywhere.'

'None the more for that he's a better example than I am. He worked hard and had his self-respect.'

'I don't want to be different. I want to be like you.'

'And so you are, more's the pity.'

One day he said, 'It's dull now the war's over.'

'That's a wicked thing to say.' Then she added, 'I suppose we spent so long looking forward to it that now there's nothing left to look forward to. Well it doesn't matter to me. I've had my day but you've got all yours to come so you'd better half start deciding what you're going to do with it.'

The trouble was he couldn't decide. There didn't seem any bent for him to follow. The thought of the various office jobs he might do made him want to spew.

'You could be a teacher,' his mother suggested and he knew that was true but what he wanted was two years before the mast like Alan Ladd or to be a Battle of Britain fighter pilot. 'Well, you'll soon enough get that wish when they call you up.' Many of the boys from the streets around were leaving school. 'Can't I leave, Mum?'

'I signed for you to stay and you'll stay till you've got a piece of paper that'll at least prove you went there.'

In the evenings when he could skive out of his homework he ran the streets with his mates who'd left, chatting up the chicks, never letting on that he was still at school. He needed money, more than his mother could give him, and scrimped on his dinner money, eating a bag of crisps in the park. There was beer to buy and the pictures to pay for. His mother got up at four to scrub offices before they opened and then went on to work in the British Restaurant dolloping out ice-cream scoops of grey mashed potato and splurging Creamola on to fruitless apple tart.

Life at school ebbed further and further from reality. It seemed a straight choice: either you went their way, the way of Crawler Edwards, or you were bolshie and went your own way, the way you'd been brought up in. Neither, it seemed to Chuff, would give him the onion-domed dream city, jewelled and loud with bells.

Even the air was restless. The papers called it demob fever. Thousands of men with gratuities and handout civvies were trying to shoehorn themselves back into a life of routine and responsibility for themselves. Chuff saw them one day in their mothers' backgardens, tanned and better fed than those who'd stopped at home, the next at the wedding, then moving out to Buckhurst Hill and setting themselves to acquire the hardwear of American dream homes. From the height of romantic teenage wisdom he decided they acquired nothing. No magic casements opened on the foam (Keats and Shelley were one of Chuff's school certificate texts). It was all forlorn like the poor bitch in the nursery rhyme who went from milking a broken-down cow to marry 'the man all tattered and torn'.

One early-closing Wednesday afternoon when he should have been up on the games field he busted a sweetshop and tobacconist the others had always said was a pushover, not realizing that the owner lived above, and was caught with his pockets stuffed with Gold Flake and his hand in the till. Chuff had kicked and struggled until the man clobbered him into submission in a chair and rang for the police.

While the law ground slowly forward Jarvis took his school certificate in a daze. In court the tobacconist told of his vicious attempts to escape. Then the homilies began. He had had every chance; the state had lavished a free education on him that he had flung back in its teeth; brave men had died for him; his mother had slaved; he was clearly unrepentant. A sharp lesson now might save him. He was remanded to an approved school for two years.

'Do you want to hear all this?' he asked as he tried to tell Philomela, his hands growing sweaty on the wheel. He had never really told anyone before, not in full.

'Yes, I want to know.'

His mother had brought him the paper saying he had passed in all subjects, with a credit in history. Chuff had been scrubbing the stone floor when she arrived, having travelled miles through the sodden winter countryside to get to the school. The news sickened him further. But he was learning.

'The boys take it in turns to go on the lam,' he said, 'but I'm passing my turn up. It's a mug's game. They catch you and bring you back and then it's worse for you.'

'Stick it out,' she said. 'I want you home proper not frightened of every knock on the door.'

When he had been home a month he was called up. 'I'll skip that bit. Everyone's soldiering's the same.' War had found him, but not the daredevil dogfights traced against a legendary summer blue. This was the infantry slog of insects and sweat through the steaming forests, without Sabu or Johnny Weissmuller to come yodelling through the trees in rescue, and the freezing stripped plateaux of winter.

The army had taught him to drive. 'Now you're home you can put it all behind you and start clean.' But what at? There was nothing he wanted to do. In desperation he got a job as a driver for a hire firm until a customer complained he wasn't wearing the uniform cap and gloves and dropping his 'sirs' in place of commas. By then he had bought his own car, beginning with a junkheap for ten quid and working his way up. Gradually other driving jobs came his way and one of these put him inside for a twelve-month stretch. When he came out he was much wiser. Now he worked only for himself and towards the really big one.

'But why the big one?' asked Philomela.

'It's the only one worth doing. Like winning the pools. It's what you're brought up on, the fairy story that one killing can make you the equal of anyone and give you the lavish style of life you want. It can be done; you're not after something that doesn't exist but something you read about other people enjoying, in the papers, all the time. If nobody had nice houses, villas on the Costa Brava, yachts, jewels, as much to eat and drink as they liked, clothes, cars, there'd be nothing to aggravate your feeling of being without. But these things exist and they're what children dream about. You know some people come into them by luck, the winning line, others are born into them, others get them by becoming pop idols or footballers.'

'What about hard work?'

'Nobody ever got anywhere by hard work without there wasn't a piece of luck or privilege tucked away somewhere. All you get from flogging your guts out day after day is enough to eat so you can go on till you flake out at sixty-five if you last that long. The dream is the big pools win, not even with hope but with just that faint possibility that helps people to go on. You talk and you think a lot in the nick. Those with a bit of clue and guts are the ones who've tried to make the dream happen. Those who aren't very bright, who get done for the petty jobs, are different. They're usually just living from hand to mouth. Society shouldn't tantalize people, hold a prize just beyond their reach while the picture show goes on of those who've got it dancing and drinking on the other side of the glass.'

'You've got it now.'

'You know I never thought of that.'

'And are you happy?'

'Too soon to tell,' said Jarvis cautiously, 'but here now, with you sitting there and smelling like a million dollars and this car under me hands, and a belly full of breakfast, yes, I'm happy here and now.'

'And violence?' Philomela said later when they'd drawn off the road into a service area with cowboy motif that caused Jarvis to christen it the hungry Fortes as he sprinkled the floor with urned coffee.

'That's different. I don't want anyone's blood on my dreams. Some of the mobsters don't care. They reckon it's them or you and anyone who gets in the way shouldn't. For them a nightwatchman's just another kind of copper. They'd say a businessman half starves and treads on people to get to the top, so what they're doing is no different.'

'What do you say though?'

'Lots of things, but they all add up to the fact that I don't hit people. There's nothing clever about violence. Any mug can be trained to kill, I saw that in the army. Besides I always have a horror that I might go to thump some poor sod of a watchman and he'd look up at me with my father's weary old mush. Call that sentimental if you like.'

'Lady Macbeth's reason for not killing the king. "Had he not resembled my father while he slept I had done't."'

'You can't, you see. Not even a bastard copper because that's his only rotten life. I don't know if I killed anyone in the army. I did me bleeding best to see they didn't kill me and I hope they were doing the same. By the way, Miss Cracknell said you were to take me over to see her and the galloping major when we got back.'

'We'd have been going anyway for the next briefing. This little number is the major's speciality.'

'No more mink farms?'

'Not now we've learned to work together,' Philomela said coolly.

*

The princess came out to meet them as the car swished to a halt. She kissed Philomela and put a hand to Jarvis. 'My dears, you've done splendidly. We got a call from our local representative. There was quite good coverage on the regional news bulletins, including a picture of the cards you left.' She clasped her hands. 'I wish I'd been there. Now you must tell me all about it.'

None of Chuff's homecomings after a job had ever been like this. His mother had never asked where he went so that she could say truthfully when they came banging on the door that she knew nothing about his business. Sometimes he would pack her off on his winnings for a holiday with Madeleine and the children. Alone in the house he would bring home a bird for the night, making sure all trace of her was gone by the time his mother got back. Not that she imagined he was a virgin or a monk but he didn't want her to get the feeling that she was only there on sufferance and had nowhere to call her own. From time to time she'd mention marriage. She didn't want to be thought one of those mothers who kept a grown-up son tied to her but he always laughed and said it should all be done away with, that the whole idea came out of the ark and he had no intention of helping to keep it afloat.

Now they sat round in the drawing room with drinks in their mitts as though the two of them were back from a few days in the Bahamas while Philomela told the story matter-of-factly, with Chuff nodding in a word or two here and there. The princess and Raphael made a responsive audience, both of them clasping their hands and exclaiming at the highlights.

'I'm afraid Althea and Alex can't be here. They're terribly disappointed but he's having one of his attacks and Althea didn't want to leave him. It's on the up turn now so it'll probably be all right for you to go over tomorrow if you'd like to telephone in the morning, Philomela dear. Now what should we do to celebrate our first success?'

'I haven't told you, but Mr Chuff is a great fan of yours. Perhaps he'd like to see some of your photographs.'

'You're very sweet, Raphael, but I don't think Mr Chuff . . .'

'Call me Jarvis, and I would, really. In fact I wondered if you'd give us a song.'

'My dears, I couldn't. The poor voice is too rusty.'

'You know this is all false modesty,' said Raphael. 'I think you should do as they ask. After all they've earned it.'

'Oh dear.' The princess looked from one to the other for confirmation.

'Please, Aunt Lottie, and put on your dress.'

'All right then, but only under duress. After dinner.'

When they took their places again Chuff saw that a small grand piano in the drawing room had been opened and the chairs slanted to face it. The princess had left them in the hall.

'You're giving her great pleasure,' said Raphael. 'She only needs to be coaxed.'

'I know,' said Philomela. 'She loves to be asked but there aren't really many opportunities these days.' Then turning to Chuff, 'You're very sweet,' she said.

To the best of his remembrance no one had ever called him 'sweet' in his life before unless it was kicking in his pram. He sat down wondering whether to be pleased or affronted and settled for pleasure since it had been Philomela's lips that had formed the word. He wondered if she had found him as sweet in bed as he had found her. It was a dangerous track to be running down in company and he put it aside till later.

'Alex will be sorry to have missed this, and Althea too,' said Raphael, handing him a glass.

'They both adore Aunt Lottie,' Philomela offered as explanation. 'Alex once asked her to marry him.'

'Shh!' whispered Raphael waving them silently to their chairs and stepping to the door which had been left slightly ajar. He must have caught some discreet off-stage signal Chuff decided, as Raphael flung the door open and stood aside to let the princess enter. There was nothing to do but applaud. 'Princess Stephanie of Balaria,' Raphael announced.

She wore a full-length dress of ivory satin bubbled with pearls, a mantle of figured brown velvet, a tiara and veil of some floating gauze. All were a little rubbed and faded so that it was as if some sepia photograph had blown from its frame into the room, the colouring of the face touched in vividly by hand as with the earliest portraits in his mother's family album where his grandmother sat nursing her first child on the studio rustic bench with his grandfather posing stiff-collared behind her.

'What shall it be?' she asked breathlessly.

'Wonderful World,' said Chuff.

'I'll try,' she said, sitting down to the piano. 'You must forgive the tremolo, my dears.'

The opening bars waltzed under her fingers and in Chuff's head the black disc began to spin, reeling away his life in an endless black thread that fell in a tangled mesh on the floor where he sat unnoticed with his mother's sewing box.

> 'World, world, wonderful world, you're mine at last!
> My lost freedom restore me, spread your wonders before me!
> Free as swallows that fly with wings unfurl'd,
> Let me wander fearlessly through the world.'

The child on the floor had thought the promise of the crescendo was to swineherds as well as princesses. Maybe a head-shrinker would say his refusal to take reality as a substitute for illusion was a sign he was a bit touched but if so then the princess and the rest of them were too, together with all nonconformists, except Philomela. Everything was 'except Philomela'.

Lottie Shoe had made reality fit illusion but it seemed to Chuff that for him the gap might be uncrossable, that as he leant over to clutch the other side it would widen as it did for the villain in cartoon films so that he was stretched thinner and thinner until finally he snapped apart. It was like the gap between the Jarvis he felt inside and the Chuff that the world saw. They too could fall apart leaving only the uninhabited space between.

The song ended with its tremble before the prolonged note calling for applause to break it. Their six hands banged together. The princess stood up and bowed while they clapped on. Then she sat down again and began to play other pieces from the score, humming and strumming together, her costume a cascade of flickering brown and opal as she flourished over the keyboard. At the end, when they clapped again for more, she closed the piano with a little laugh and gave her hand to Raphael who led her to a chair.

His pink room welcomed him back. This, Chuff thought as he undressed, must be what it was like to come back from boarding school for the holidays. He tried to imagine Philomela in her room along the corridor but he had never been inside and his imagination floundered. Tomorrow he must take a quick looksee. Instead he let his mind play through yesterday again. It had been good and he had been desperate but not as good he reckoned as they might be when she knew him better. He felt her hands caressing his back again as he sank deep into her, stroking his arse so that small currents ran from her fingertips through his flesh and he had to hold on tight not to come too soon and it all be over with before he'd really had time to enjoy himself. As he remembered he wanted her again.

Had she liked him? She had said so but that was before. He wondered how he compared with the others she'd had. He wanted to be best, of course, but who wouldn't? He laughed at himself as he cleaned his teeth. Would she let him again or was it once only? Well, he would have to change her mind if that was what she thought, he swaggered, trying out words and stances in his head, thrusting his thumbs in the waistband of his trousers to draw her attention, staring her down into sensuality. Slipping a hand inside his underpants he cupped his equipment soothingly in his hand and drifted towards sleep.

'Over to the major then?' Chuff said as they set out in the morning.

'It's not far. Turn right outside the drive.'

'As long as I'm not expected to go by horse.'

'That's the short way. It's longer by road.' Even so they were turning into a private lane in a few minutes, the car bouncing on the unmade surface.

'Althea bought this place to be near Aunt Lottie. I think they met in the war when Althea was driving ambulances and Aunt Lottie entertaining the troops.'

'It's not the major's?'

'No, she's the one with the money. She's a genius with stocks and shares. She has to do it all through a broker of course but he just does what he's told. She's made a fortune. It's mainly her money we're using.'

The Rover ground on under dripping leafless trees until the lane took a last turn and ended in front of a large square farmhouse flanked by out-buildings. Philomela pulled the bell and the door was opened by a manservant whose every move and inflexion suggested regular army to Chuff. Miss Althea was in the stables; the major in the morning room. Philomela led them through the house towards the out-houses.

Althea, looking like a training jockey in her boots, trousers and polo-necked sweater, cropped white hair pushed back from her forehead and a pail in one hand, came towards them from the central block followed by a handsome piebald horse, a greyhound and a sheep. 'I've nearly finished. Then I'll join you for a conference.' She seemed more at ease out here than in the princess's drawing room. 'Delilah, say good morning.' The horse bowed back on its haunches and raised a forefoot. Then it stood upright and nudged Althea in the back. Absentmindedly she produced a piece of apple from her pocket and fed it between the thick yellow tombstones of teeth. 'She likes sugar lumps best but they're bad for her. Used to be a circus horse. Show him round, Philly, and then find Alex. He's much better this morning.'

'These are Althea's refugees,' said Philomela as she led him into the straw-and-animal-smelling complex of barns and stables. 'She rescues them and rehabilitates them and then finds homes for as many as possible.'

'I thought there were societies for doing that sort of thing.'

'So there are, but they can't cope with the numbers. Eventually if homes can't be found the animals have to be killed. The greyhound was a racer who was too old to run any more; the sheep, an orphan and sickly.'

'Althea had a little lamb.'

'People bring animals to her from miles around. There's a donkey and a goat in a field at the back and a racehorse that was going to be shot after a fall. Althea ran on to the course and knocked the gun up. It was in a bellysling for months while the leg mended.'

There seemed to be at least some of everything; cats, white mice, rats, hamsters, some boxes of straw that Philomela said hid hibernating tortoises, a run of rabbits, a fox and a scrabble of chickens picking in their own hedged enclosure. 'It's like those farmyards of lead animals we had as kids,' said Chuff. 'They were always plump and glossy like this lot.' Until the war came and they started to make them out of plastic and paste and they got flat and scrawny with their features clumsily blobbed in. That was when he grew out of them. 'Who was the bloke on the door?'

'Alex's batman.'

'I thought I smelt blanco.'

The major, looking a little more frail than before and with a travelling rug round his legs, leant forward over his stick and said, 'Corton.'

'The weapons research place?' Chuff asked amazed. 'That's a bit of a jump up on letting our furcoats take to the hills, isn't it?'

'Escalation,' the major said firmly. 'It's time to really worry them, let them realize we mean business.'

'I don't see how it comes in unless they're teaching monkeys to fly A-bombers these days or man the midget subs.'

'Every weapon is tested on animals first: nerve gases, radiation, napalm. But it's not just the place itself, it's as a symbol of the whole field of research in which animals are used as, one might say, guinea pigs. Millions of them every year, subject to the will of sadists in white coats who've never got over the desire to pull wings off butterflies. I'd horsewhip the lot, I'd . . .'

'Now Alex, you know what Lottie says.'

The major sighed. 'Anyway you don't have to be convinced. You just have to . . .'

'Carry out orders?' asked Chuff.

'Something like that.'

'And what are they?'

'Destroy the labs.'

'Won't there be some animals in them if what you say is true?'

'Yes. We have to face that. But those that are will be doomed already. We'll just be putting them out of their misery.'

'I take it you've got plans of the buildings and some suggestions?'

'Yes,' said the major. 'This is my special baby. Pull this one off for me and I can die happy.'

'These plans,' said Chuff, 'suggest you've got an inside contact.' The question had been worrying him ever since the princess had mentioned a local representative. The major nodded agreement. Talking seemed to tire him today. 'More than one?'

'Do you mean inside Corton?'

'I mean in general, anywhere.'

'There is an organization if that's what you're asking.'

'I think I should be told the full story.'

The major looked at Philomela. 'I think he should,' she said. It came to Chuff that she had been doing an undercover job on him in more ways than one.

'Very well. If Philomela thinks so. The organization is like Chinese boxes. No doubt you know that the whole animal welfare movement is quite big. It's divided into lots of societies each with its own particular sphere of activity. Each group thinks its own horror is the worst and works to end it. Put them all together and you have a total picture of exploitation and death that can only be ended by a complete change of attitude and legislation; not only here but all over the world. Within this mass of workers there are some who see the overall picture and, within those, some who realize that the situation is deteriorating even further, as man's standard of living rises at the expense of the other species. Within that central group All Heaven In A Rage has arisen. It has two parts: those of us that you know who are the angels and an outer ring of those who are prepared to be used in limited ways, who are the cherubim. When our example succeeds here it will be followed in other countries until there is international agreement.'

'The lion shall kip down with the lamb,' said Chuff. 'These

cherubim, can they be relied on not to talk? Suppose they get questioned?'

'They know only a tiny part but that part would incriminate themselves not anyone else. Therefore they'll keep quiet.'

'You don't have too high an opinion of people.'

'If man weren't vicious and greedy above all other species this situation wouldn't have arisen.'

'Coming from a professional soldier, which I take it you were, that makes strange hearing.'

'I fought my fellows because they were just what I've said. Only Lottie gave me some hope that they might be changed, by fear and self-interest. That's the only thing men understand. Our cherub in Corton is a lab assistant sickened by the things he's been asked to do. He doesn't know the identity of any of the rest. You see,' the major smiled, 'I was in intelligence; I know how it's done, how a network is organized.'

He was glad to get away, to be alone for a bit and try to sort things out in his own mind. The thought that Philomela had been sizing him up disturbed his vanity. He had begun to think she might like him for himself and now it seemed as if she'd just been doing a job on him. How much had been put on, he wondered. He'd read about women who could fake a climax, did it for years, and sometimes a brass, if she thought it'd bring in a bit more, would put on an act. Then again there were some you could hardly tell with. There'd been one who'd kept her eyes shut all the time and at the crunch she'd turned her head sideways and screwed up her face a bit so you hardly knew if there was anything going on in there at all. Philomela had been there, he was almost sure, but suppose she'd just felt randy, it wouldn't have mattered who it was, and she'd been able to kill two birds with one fuck. He flung himself on the pink bed in a petulant ache.

There was no reason why she should like him, a failed con who'd been picked out of the pen like a fish on a line to be the skivvy of a bunch of upper-class loonies. Maybe she'd got a special kick out of having it off with a villain. She could tell the story at dinner parties. Beyond the bar and the distorting pane the voices surged and broke in combers of laughter against the smoke-darkened wood. A childish melancholy sent him to the window to brood on the landscape that fumed with rain again. It would never be spring. They had locked it up in some leaden winter nick and would hold the countryside to ransom for it till it disgorged Jarvis Chuff, throw him back inside where he would never see Philomela again.

> At night when I am sleeping I have a pleasant dream
> With my true love I am strolling down by some . . . stream
> Through England I am roaming with her at my command
> Then waken broken-hearted all on Van Diemen's Land.

What was it? 'Wandering'? 'Pleasant'? No, 'purling'. That was it. He remembered now. In his first stretch there had been a chap who had sung it at a cons' concert. Afterwards Jarvis had asked him about it, if the bloke had made it up himself and he'd said no, it was an old poacher's song like 'The Lincolnshire Poacher' and Jarvis remembered that from singing at school and from *Tom Brown's Schooldays*. It had always used to make him angry, now suddenly it gave him a lump in the throat.

Come all you gallant poachers that ramble free from care
That walk out of a moonlit night with your dog, your gun, your snare
Where the lofty hare and pheasant you have at your command
Not thinking that your last career is on Van Diemen's Land.

He had been proud and angry for the gallant poachers, 'trepanned by the Keeper's hideous hand', sent down and transported for fourteen years, though they were lucky not to be topped in those days. Now he thought about the 'lofty hare and pheasant'. He'd seen them sitting upright in the moonlight before they were bowled over, but they were 'lofty' too because they were some nob's private property and more valuable than the singer. But not their own sake because the nob would be out with his beaters and his pals to knock them over when he was ready. That made them and the poacher about equal.

The singer had dreamed of having the pheasant and his bird at his command, supposedly for knocking off whenever he wanted. At that moment Jarvis felt anything but in command.

There was a tap on the door. He turned from the window to answer it. Philomela was standing in the corridor. Chuff felt himself blinking at her.

'I'm sorry, were you asleep?'

He could hardly breathe. His pulse was knocking and he felt sick as a dog. He was falling, falling for a lofty bird while she laughed at him and, no doubt, would see him shopped when he'd served their purpose. Well he would walk away any day, into the nearest copshop and be welcomed with the red carpet, take his ache back inside with him and bury it in that fortress until the years sealed the wound with dust. That choice was still his.

'Are you all right?'

'Don't I look it?'

'You look as if you've been seeing ghosts.'

'Christmas yet to come, I expect. Is there something I can do for you, lady?'

'You'd stopped calling me that.'

'Perhaps I shouldn't have.'

'What is it?' She looked at him questioningly. 'Is it something I've done?'

'Oh Jesus,' he said reaching for her. 'Yes, it's something you've done.' He didn't go much on kissing birds as a rule, but he was going to kiss this one.

'Do you think,' she asked when he let her speak, 'that we ought to make some plans?'

'I could just ride up to the gate, bang on the gong conveniently left hanging there by kind permission of J. Arthur Rank and wait for someone to come out and fight. Then I could get a job in pictures.'

'I think,' said Philomela, 'we should do something about your interesting pallor.'

'I know. I look as if I crawled out from under a stone.'

'We'll put you under the sunlamp. I think too, you should grow a little toothbrush moustache. We'll grey you up a bit to make you look older.

'Make me just like the major in fact.'

'That's right.'

'We'll need ID. He'll have to fix that and a green car with flashes. Get someone to buy one so we can knock it off, and ditch it later. Let's have a look at those plans again.' There were aerial photographs as well as a groundplan. 'It's a monstrous great place; almost a town on its own. That'll work on our side I think. There must be lots of people wandering about since so many of them live on the site. We shan't be able to do more than token damage, I reckon, depending on how small they can pack a big blast. But it'll be enough to make them take notice.'

He looked at himself in the mirror. Major Chuff looked back. It was frightening how quickly you could become someone else. Public schools: Eton and Spewed-Up. He pushed up the brim of his hardtop cap with his swagger-stick and cocked an eyebrow. That's how he'd have looked by now if he'd signed on. Not so long in the tooth of course. The grizzling of hair and moustache and the accentuation of crowsfeet with tanning gave him an extra ten years. But much the same. If he'd been able to accept it in the first place that's what he'd have hardened into. Was that it then? The first decision led by inevitable metamorphosis to a predictable end, chrysalis to moth, and even Crawler Edwards wasn't to blame for his outcome. Yet he was, Jarvis was sure. He'd made the first step. Then the process had begun to work on him. But every day when he got up he had to make a decision to go on being what he had become. You could opt out at any moment as Jarvis could have opted in. When he'd done his time in the army he could have signed on for longer, gone for an officer. All would have been forgiven: bright boy decides to make good. Then it would have begun; the slow winching him away from Thaxsted Street up towards the light while she receded further below him, smiling as she drowned. He saw her face set in a swirl of black water or smoke as the train drew out taking him, labelled for evacuation, with the taste of cinders in his mouth.

He took off his uniform jacket and packed the top of Major Chuff into his suitcase. The moustache prickled his fingers with its newness like grey flannel shorts at the beginning of the September term. Philomela was waiting downstairs, already wearing her green uniform under a macintosh, her hair swept up ready for the forage cap.

'Listen,' he said as he drove west along the A4. 'I want to say something to you very serious.'

'Yes,' she said demurely. He wondered if she was laughing at him.

'If we're caught or rather if I'm caught you're to get out if you can. No false heroics, see? If we're both caught you're to save yourself. They'll give you bail and you're to jump it. Leave the country.'

'And what about you?'

'They won't trust me with bail so the question doesn't arise. They'll throw the book at us, conspiracy, treason I shouldn't wonder, the lot; and they'll have me in the strong box so fast me feet won't touch the ground, but they won't know about you. They'll set bail high but whoever's financing this lot won't mind coughing up.'

'But . . .'

'There won't be anything you can do for me either way, get that clear, and it won't make me feel any better, in fact a whole sight worse, to think of you cosily stitching mailbags in Holloway.'

'If we're caught the angels will try to get us out. They promised you that.'

'Oh they'll try, I grant you, but knowing how I was sprung before, I wouldn't be surprised if they pass an Act to put me in the Tower; anything to keep me safe. So no heroics.'

But all Philomela would say was: 'We'll see,' and she set her face stubbornly. 'We shall just have to make sure we're not caught.' Chuff hoped it was a more personal concern than a sense of justice.

His papers said *Major Gabriel, Intelligence*. 'A very distinguished military family,' the real major had commented, 'principally in the Indian service. Do you think you can live up to it?'

'If I talk with a plum in me mouth and a cold in me nose.'

The dark green saloon was parked in a lane beside an old quarry, converted to a reservoir, where they had expected to find it. They left their own car, fixed on the plastic transfer flashes, adjusted their uniforms and drove off, Philomela at the wheel, Major Gabriel lounging in the back. Soon they were running beside the perimeter fence with its warning notices. Chuff's ears began their usual highwire song of fear like telegraph lines on a hot still day. The car swung in through the main entrance and drew up at the glass box housing the security officer. Chuff got out swiftly and went in while the guard was still pushing himself to his feet. He flipped his ID open on the table. 'Come to look at your security, spot check. Chief security officer, where do I find him?'

'I'll just ring through, sir.'

'No need. Tell my driver where to go.' He walked out, back to the car. Philomela was standing with the door open. Chuff flung himself into the back seat and she shut the door on him. She was wearing glasses; her hair was pinned frumpishly under her cap.

'If you take the main avenue, miss, and turn left, the office is three blocks along.'

Philomela drew off smoothly. They had come just far enough for her to be used to the car. 'He's gone back in,' she said, following the guard in the driving mirror. They turned the corner out of sight of the glass box.

'He'll be ringing through to let them know we're coming. You okay?'

'Yes.'

They passed a husband and wife laden with Saturday afternoon shopping and a toddler – boy or girl, you couldn't tell – in pink eskimo outfit like a Christmas cake decoration. The child looked up at the car with a gleam of complicity. 'This is it.' They stopped in front of an office block that looked as if it had been hastily thrown up from children's too-red building bricks. Chuff sprang out. 'Half an hour, corporal.'

'Yes, sir,' Philomela verbally saluted and swung the car away. Chuff doubled up the steps into an outer officer, already speaking as the boy behind the desk got to his feet. 'I take it your chap on the gate rang through. Now where's your number one, Mr Billings?'

The answering stutter was cut short by a side door opening.

'Mr Billings?' said Chuff starting forward with a hand out. 'Gabriel, special group.'

'I'm afraid Mr Billings has gone to London for the day. I'm Mortimer. If I can help . . .'

'Oh, that's damned awkward.'

'If you'd let me know, sir . . .'

'That's the whole point. Well, we'd better go in.' Chuff pushed through into the office. Mortimer took the chair behind the desk in an attempt to regain the initiative.

'As you know,' Chuff said leaning back, 'we don't like to interfere, prefer to let you run your own concerns but we're picking up a lot of chatter from different sources that suggests you're on the list for a job of some sort.'

'Really, sir? Isn't there always a lot of talk like that? It never comes to anything. A few demonstrators shout about in front but the dogs stop them getting over the wire.'

'My dear lad, you don't think I'd waste my time if it was just the usual gossip. You mustn't let familiarity breed contempt you know. You'll look pretty damn silly if we bother to warn you and then you get done.' Mortimer shifted uncomfortably. With relief Chuff saw that the man had written him off as an old woman.

'Have you any idea what these people might be after, sir?'

'Not yet but if we so hear, we'll let you know. Now if you could just give me a quick whisk round. I've told my corporal half an hour.'

'I don't think I could . . .'

Chuff got to his feet wearily. 'I'm sorry you feel like that.'

'Really there's nothing to see. The boffins have all gone home. The alarms are set. There are our men at their different points . . .'

'And the dogs,' Chuff said satirically. 'Really you chaps must think it's the Middle Ages.' Mortimer's face was wooden with suppressed anger. 'I shall have to report of course. You might tell Mr Billings I called, and mention our worries.' He heaved himself out of the chair. 'I'll be in touch.' Mortimer followed him into the outer room where the receptionist stumbled to his feet again. Through the window Chuff saw Philomela swing into position. He marched out of the office, stepped up to the door and waited for her to open it.

'We've got about eight minutes. How did it go?' he asked as soon as they were moving.

'The whole block's deserted. It backs on to the fence and the wood as we thought, so no one should get hurt. I managed to leave the car and nip round the back, for a smoke if anyone asked, but no one did. The door's there. I found the alarm and clamped on that gadget for bypassing it without breaking the circuit. It must be all right or you'd have heard all the bells ringing in the office. There are the laboratories.'

They had driven away from the residential blocks and there was no one about. 'The guard will be round in fifteen minutes,' Chuff said looking at his watch. 'Keep the engine running. If anything goes wrong get the hell out.' He opened the back door and stepped out on the road, carrying an attaché case and feeling for his keys. The door was there at the back of the laboratory block as Philomela had said and he could see the junction she had fitted. Now to find out if it worked. Gently Chuff tried his keys on the service door, holding his breath as the lock turned on the third and he pushed inside, half expecting bells to shrill out all round him, but nothing happened. The next door was a simple swing. These weren't the labs where the heavy stuff went on. They had decided against those as too potentially dangerous, capable of loosing a poisonous miasma, a blast of contaminating dragon's breath into the air. But there were animals here. He caught a skittering of dry feet on cage floors. He approached carefully. There were rats and rabbits along one wall, their flanks showing the fungoid spread of gas burns.

He pushed through another door, holding the case in front of him. 'They're all doomed anyway,' the major had said. This time he didn't look in the cages but out of the corner of his eye he caught a series of boxes from which white rabbit heads protruded, turning on their coffins, their eyes bandaged. Chuff opened the case, found an empty cupboard, set the dial for three o'clock in the morning and began to back out.

Outside he closed the door, removed the junction and, walking calmly back to the car, got into the back seat. 'Done,' he said as Philomela moved off. 'Let's shift.' They left by a secondary gate where the keeper made no attempt to stop them, swung round in a wide arc and headed back for the reservoir. Dusk was falling rapidly. Philomela drew up behind their own car. The lane was still deserted. They changed hastily, bundling their uniforms into the boot of the green saloon. Chuff shaved his moustache with a few quick passes in the driving mirror. Philomela unpinned her hair.

'You watch out on the road,' he said. 'I'll ditch the car. If anyone comes past they'll think I've gone for a slash.'

She opened the gate to the field and closed it when he had driven through. 'If anything happens give me a toot.'

While she went back to the Rover, Jarvis positioned the green saloon on a bank above the now-dark water. The soggy surface held the wheels while he crept out. Then he put his shoulder to the back and heaved. Nothing happened. Jarvis swore. If he'd wanted it to stick there it would have been in the water by now. Turning his back on it he strained his legs to walk the heavy car, digging his heels in hard. With a small sucking sound it suddenly began to go, nearly dropping him on his back. For a second it tilted and then nose-dived into the water with a huge echoing splash, turning turtle and settling quickly. The water was about six feet deep and covered the wheels but it was easy to see that something big had gone in. Perhaps by the time someone thought to search the reservoir it would be less obvious. Chuff ran down the bank. He wanted to get away from the desolation of the mud-walled wet lead water where a night wind was beginning to sough in whispers as the temperature dropped, and from the drowned car with its reproachful wheels setting fast in the water, back to the warmth and smell of Philomela.

As he opened the door the mingled scent of her perfume and a fresh cigarette flowed out, wrapping and soothing him. Jarvis found he was shivering. He had sweated over the car's burial and the sweat had grown quickly cold. 'The bugger wouldn't shift at first but it's gone now, committed to the deep. Is there something in the flask? It's getting a bit parky out there. I feel as if I've got rising damp,' he heard himself running on as he reached for a drink. 'Do we have to go back now?'

'No,' said Philomela. 'Not if you don't want to.'

'Then let's go somewhere.'

'I'll ring Aunt Lottie to tell her we're quite safe and then I'll drive you to somewhere for dinner.'

'No,' Chuff said, beginning to feel better, 'I'll drive you and we'll got to Brighton.'

'Yes major,' she said and took the slip road for the M4.

'That's all right,' said Philomela, coming back from the telephone booth to where Jarvis sat in the darkened car parked on the service forecourt. He had decided against a cup of motorway tea feeling naked without moustache. Vulnerability had set in as he watched her walking into the lit glasshouse in search of a phone. If they once got even the breath of an idea that Chuff, escapee, was running around in a flash car with an even flasher bird, if they should ever put two and two together and make five of it, deciding that was what he was doing with money to burn, or some copper with a photographic memory get a snap on his wanted mug, remember the rogues' gallery on the station wall and realize that Britain's most popular figure wasn't wintering abroad, then they would all be hallooing after him up and down the country and he wouldn't dare show his red face outside his foxhole. There would be nothing to connect him with this particular caper; it was too far outside his usual fields of activity. But if he was caught in the act he would get twenty or thirty years and that meant he would probably never come out at all. So he mustn't be caught, and if he was he must make a run for it somehow, with or without the angels being on his side. Relief swept through him at Philomela's figure, backed by light, walking towards his shadowed patch of ground.

'The call will be made at eight minutes to three. We have Aunt Lottie's blessing for Brighton.'

Jarvis took over the driving and they turned towards Kingston. His silence lay like a third presence between them. Desperately he tried to think of something that would break it but everything was either too harsh or a whimper. Suddenly he said: 'If your Aunt Lottie was married to a prince who was your father's cousin, what does that make him to you?'

Philomela smiled. 'Does it worry you?'

'I don't know. It might, I suppose. Depends on the answer.'

'Then perhaps I shouldn't tell you.'

'I just want to know whether I should be calling you your ladyship, or something.'

'If you want to be technical it's *gräfin*.'

'Come again?'

'It's the feminine of *graf*.'

'Like Graf Spee?'

'That's right. It means count.'

'Countess then?' Jarvis saw her nod. 'I thought you'd be at least a princess too.'

'Are you disappointed?'

'It was meant to be a joke.'

'Technically you're right.' She drew an ember glow from her cigarette. 'My father was a prince but he didn't approve of titles that didn't mean anything. He liked to be realistic and adapt himself, not like so many of his acquaintances who couldn't adapt and either committed suicide in one sense or another or became spongers.'

'What about the countess lark? Is that still on then?'

'In a way. The prince bit is just a hereditary title that doesn't mean anything but there are theoretically estates in Russia and Germany I could try to lay claim to if I fancied a term in Siberia or on a collective farm.'

'Why Russia?'

'Do you really want the boring story of my family tree?'

'Why not?'

'Well, when Catherine the Great came from Germany in the eighteenth century she invited thousands of Germans to settle on the Volga.'

'Song of the Vulgar boatmen, yes?'

'That's it. One of my ancestors was among them. Catherine gave him an estate. I believe he was quite a favourite of hers at one time.'

'Who wasn't?'

'English puritan. Anyway during the First World War the German population was deeply suspected and the emperor ordered their destruction but the revolution came just in time. They made themselves into a German Workers' Commune. That was when my father decided to leave.'

'Didn't like his land being shared out among the peasants?'

'No, it wasn't that. He was only young and he'd never liked it on the estate in the country. He'd joined the army, although he didn't have to, and he thought there was going to be a lot of fighting and misery so he decided to continue his education in Europe. In Biarritz he met my mother who was on holiday with her family. Then he invited himself to stay with his cousin Prince Ferdinand so that he could follow her to England and persuade her to marry him.'

'It's a fairy story. What happened to the estates?'

'The area became a German Republic in the twenties. Stalin abolished it during the Second World War and deported all those of German descent to Siberia.'

'Just like the Tsar. So what does that make you?'

'Heinz fifty-seven varieties I should think. The original count married a Russian. There's some French somewhere and my mother was Anglo-Irish.'

It all took a bit of swallowing and Jarvis tried hard as they drove through the underpass at Gatwick with the sound of a jet warming up to drown out their own engines. The strangeness of it glowed in his head like the never-to-be-attained Moscow of his dreams, the pantomime transformation scene, the opening in the hill that led always to a palace carved from a single lump of crystal whose windows were sapphires, rubies and emeralds. Yet it was a life that someone, flesh and blood father of Philomela, sitting where he could touch her, had really lived.

'What was he like?'

'My father. It's hard to say, isn't it?'

'What did he do, or didn't he have to do anything?'

'He worked very hard at translating and at running a publishing firm that specialized in foreign books. It meant that he spent a lot of time abroad so I stayed with Aunt Lottie during the holidays.'

There were so many questions he wanted to ask about what had happened to all the people in this exotic drama, that read a bit like the plot of *The Balkan Princess* itself, that he didn't know where to start and anyway some of it might be painful. He noticed she didn't ask him anything in return but then he had nothing interesting to tell, no storybook once upon a time of princes. Jack and the Beanstalk was more his tale, except that in his version the giant caught Jack and put him in a cage from which he had to be rescued ignominiously by a princess.

'What would you have done if you'd ever got a lot of money?' Philomela asked suddenly.

'Spent it, like anyone else. After my mother died I could have gone off anywhere; Majorca for instance.'

'Do you think you ever can?'

'What?'

'Walk out on yourself.'

'Is it yourself you're brought up with? Can't you ever get away? Is that what you mean? If you can't it isn't fair, is it, that people should be brought up so differently. You here and me there, so that we can't ever meet.'

'We seem to have met,' Philomela said.

'Yeah, but it had to be a bloody big coincidence to bring it off.'

They ate what Chuff couldn't bring himself to think of as dinner on the outskirts of Brighton in a red plush and mahogany-veneered restaurant with Italian boys in penguin suits. When Jarvis mentioned his difficulty with the naming of meals Philomela said: 'You're a class puritan like all the English.'

'What does that mean?'

'That every class in England thinks its own is the most virtuous and that to cross the barriers is to break some great taboo like marrying your sister. It makes everyone from another class forbidden and exciting. And you can all pick each other out by your clothes, accent, walk so that you could estimate precisely what someone's parents were, what they earned, where the person was educated and so on down to the very pictures they have on the wall. Secretly you're proud of the whole mumbo-jumbo like other people are proud of their religious differences.'

'I thought according to the papers and the telly it was all disappearing and we're becoming a classless society.'

'Like hell,' said Philomela. 'Ten per cent of you may be; the ten per cent of middle-class liberals who can afford it can now be free of all the other classes as pop stars and disc jockeys and let their children mix with the working classes at school knowing that their own home culture and their incomes can lift their children out if they ever seriously look like becoming factory hands.'

'And what about you?'

'I just like some people more than others.'

He wanted to ask her then if he was one of them but he was too afraid of the answer. Philomela had ordered a cheese omelet after her gondola of melon with its oar of a cochineal cherry on a stick. Jarvis looked down the list. 'Could I have one of those too?'

'You don't have to just because I do.'

'No, but I fancy it.' Suddenly he felt a little sick.

'You've gone very white. What's the matter?'

'Suppose something goes wrong and someone gets hurt?'

'It can't. You know Alex has got an observer there to make sure no one's near and the call will just give them time to ring through if there is any slip but not time to dispose of the bomb. But no one ever is there at that time; that was checked again and again.' Philomela was perfectly cool and rational. She kept her voice low. Chuff watched her speaking, hardly hearing the words but letting the tones flow over him as if he was lying in the shallows on a summer day with each small incoming wave lifting his legs and pushing him a little up the sand. 'You're not listening.'

'It's not that.' He began to dig holes with the tiny spoon in the miniature salt pan but they wouldn't stay. The dry grains tumbled like hourglass sand, constantly filling his excavations. 'I didn't want to tell you but there were animals in there, quite a lot of them. Some had burns and some had bandages over their eyes. Rabbits and rats mostly.'

'They test gas effects on the eyes like that. Except that rabbits can't cry so they can't weep the gas away like we might.'

'Jesus, bloody brer rabbits.'

'Isn't that sentimental?'

'Yeah, I suppose it is but that's part of the way it took me. I've been trying to decide if I was like them, already boxed up with things burning me eyes out, not understanding anything, would I be glad to be put out of me misery? Would I still want to go on fighting to stay alive? I don't know if I'm a murderer or the doctor with the needle to take all the pain and fear away. Animals don't think like we do, but they must have an instinct to go on living, that's what we call hope. And all those burns. Someone must have made them quite calmly, knowing more or less what would happen.'

'Isn't that exactly what happens in war? Bombs are dropped and bullets fired and so on, knowing more or less what will happen.'

'Yeah but somehow this seemed even more cold-blooded. The people who're doing it don't come near the end products or their use. They're just ... just playing at it somehow, without any of the excuse of it being you or him. And yet a part of me knew how it felt, how it was possible to do something like that. It's a feeling I remember from somewhere. You think you're being all detached and clinical just observing but underneath you're enjoying it.' Suddenly he saw the biology lab on a wet afternoon, with the stink of formalin, the tears down the sooty panes and the cold tough flesh of the frog he was dissecting. He stood at the draining board while his mother held down the lengths of wet black eel and cut off the squirming heads. 'Do they really die at sunset, Mum?' 'So they say. But we never leave them that long.' 'Can I do one?' 'Hold it tight then.'

With the memory pinned down he felt better. 'What does Philomela mean?' he asked.

For the first time he seemed to have caught her off guard. 'Do you want both meanings?'

'If there are two.'

'One is "the nightingale" after a Greek story of a girl who was changed into a nightingale.'

'And the other?'

'I'm afraid it means "beloved".'

'There's a handle. Who thought that one up?'

'My father, I'm afraid.'

'What happened to Philomela in the story?'

'She had her tongue cut out among other things, so I rather hope there's nothing in a name.'

*

The flat plane of sea glittered below them. They had parked the car on the grassed cliff verge and sat looking towards the dark horizon. Away on the right the pier lights were strung like a liner motionless at anchor. Jarvis had taken one of Philomela's cigarettes so that there should be two small lamps in the car. 'As if it was a lighthouse,' he had said. He knew what he wanted, wanted badly.

'Do we have to go back at all tonight?'

'What did you have in mind?'

Was she teasing him again? 'I should have thought that was obvious.'

'I don't come with the job, you know,' she said calmly. 'I'm not just part of the bonus.'

'I'm sorry. I can't help it.'

'I'm sorry too that we can't lay you on something more interesting, someone who could be sent off afterwards, but it's too dangerous.'

'You didn't seem to mind last time,' he stabbed at himself.

'So you thought that as we'd just finished another job I might be available again?'

'Are you making out I'm bleeding kinky; that I only come on when I've done a job?'

'No. I think you probably want it most of the time. I'm not an object you know, nor a sex machine. You could buy one of those rubber dollies with the hole in the right place and two inflatable breasts.'

He wanted to hit her then, to give her a real gob full of fist that'd smash the words back down her throat, and he wanted to pull her out on the cold grass and ram it in hard until she cried out with pleasure and pain together. He pounded his clenched hand on the padded fascia top.

'All right, all right, you made your point. I'm sorry I didn't come up to scratch. Why don't you write on me report "Can do better with more effort"?'

'Are you trying to hurt yourself or me?'

'Bleeding women!'

'Why don't you say "middle-class women", then you can kill two birds with one go. Flash your working-class virility.'

'Lady,' he said, 'you can get arrested for that.' He put out a finger and stroked the back of her hand where it rested on her lap. His anger was gone now, almost as if he had fucked her. Jarvis switched on the engine and bumped the car off the grass. Far out a real beacon was flashing beyond where sea and sky became one blue-black wash.

'The trouble is,' he said, 'I don't want a rubber dolly, I want you.'

'Me or . . .'

'You,' he put in smartly.

'Good,' she said.

'Pardon?'

'I hoped you might.'

'Then what was all that palaver about?'

'I wanted to be sure and make you sure. As a matter of fact I told Aunt Lottie I didn't think we'd be back till tomorrow.'

'To think you can break the law just lying in bed,' Jarvis said.

'Don't boast,' Philomela murmured sleepily.

'That's not a boast,' he said putting his arms akimbo under his head. He couldn't remember when he'd felt so bloody marvellous.

'Then you're trying to make me blush and I'm not awake enough for that.'

'Oi, you with the face on,' Jarvis said tenderly, 'look at me.' Philomela opened one eye. 'I like you a lot.'

'Yes, funny Chuff, I like you too.' The eye closed.

'That's all right then.' In a minute he would get up and make some tea or coffee but for a moment he savoured the gently breathing warmth of Philomela beside him. If this room with its bed in it could be loosed from its moorings in time and space and drift off into forever then he would be entirely content.

'Except that we should get hungry,' she said when he put it to her.

'A maid could knock from time to time with a tray of something and then step on to a passing cloud and float away. What's the good of being an angel if you can't order little things like that.' He swung his feet to the floor. It was too early for the papers but there was the news he could listen to while the kettle boiled. 'Shall we see if they say anything on the wireless?' Philomela sat up and reached for her cigarettes. He knew now what she was like under the nightdress, knew every part of her and the knowledge increased rather than slackened his wanting. Their smell mingled on his body. For once he found himself walking about naked, without self-consciousness, perhaps because he was still so conscious of her body under and round him.

He paused in his trek to the bathroom. 'At three o'clock this morning a medium-sized bomb exploded in the laboratories at Corton, the government research establishment. The block was badly damaged but no one was injured. The incident is said to be the work of a pressure group who telephoned Corton that a bomb had been planted. Telephone calls were also received by several national newspapers warning that this was only the second of a series of planned terrorist actions to force the government and the United Nations to consider an international charter for animals. However, a government spokesman suggested that this might be a cover for other activities of a politcal nature. It has not escaped notice that the initials of the organization, AHIAR, are very close to those of the IRA.'

'Bloody cheek!' said Chuff, switching off. 'Suggesting we're a branch of the IRA. What do they mean by "terrorist" anyway?'

'I thought you were only the hired hand,' said Philomela. 'You're getting involved.'

'Don't get cheeky or I shall have to deal with you again.'

Philomela wriggled down into the bed, letting a plume of smoke drift up towards the ceiling to shimmer in milky wreaths where a shaft of sunlight fingered between the curtains. 'We shall be too late for breakfast if you don't let me get up soon.'

'Bloody women,' said Chuff with pleasure and shut himself in the bathroom, hugging the thought that when he came out she would still be there.

'There was a lot they didn't tell the public,' Jarvis said. The angels were in conference in the princess's drawing room. 'You must call me Lottie,' she had said to Chuff. They had told their story of the expedition to an admiring audience. The major had been particularly delighted.

'If it had been a full military establishment instead of one of these hybrids you mightn't have got away with it. The trouble is they know there are two of you, one of each, if you take my meaning, and that's something it's hard to disguise. It may become necessary to take along some cover.'

'You're just trying to get into the act, Alex,' said Philomela.

'Even vicarious action seems to do me good. I feel ten years younger and healthier today.'

Raphael wagged his finger. 'We must all remember about pride and a fall and that we have a long way to go. What's our next target?'

'There's a big slaughterhouse that I think we should attend to. Hit the commercial boys, and soon, so the authorities have no chance to get their breath back. We must keep up our calls to the press too so that they can't ignore us.'

It was a bit like VE day, Jarvis thought. At any moment they would be getting out the trestle tables for the street parties and lighting the bonfires. His mother had seen he was home in time for theirs. The Japs were still fighting but that wasn't the same, more the Yanks' concern and the sense of victory hadn't been smeared with atomic death. They had borrowed the benches and tables from the mission where his mother had gone to the Band of Hope bunfights when she was his age and set the street out like a banqueting hall under a black basin of sky flushed with the night glow of the city. For weeks there had been house-to-house collections, lashed out now in beer and prize money for the street sports. The beer made them gentle and nostalgic as if all the years of aggression were being washed away in the booze-up that didn't end in a barney. The smoke from the bonfire made their eyes swim. It was all Guy Fawkeses and family kneesups fat with singing aunts as the voices rose up round the fiery skeletons of old furniture burning like in a great crucible with their incendiary echo tamed. He drank in the smell of malt and the hot pavements and woodsmoke, summer larded over with autumn, and knew he must remember it always, that it would never happen again. Later when they read Tennyson's *Morte d'Arthur* he couldn't pin down why the end always gave him an ache in the throat beyond what belonged to the words.

> And I, the last, go forth companionless
> And the days darken round me, and the years
> Among new men, strange faces, other minds.

But the songs they sang were mostly from the Great War, and earlier even, as if they had been besieged for half a century or in a trance where time stood still for them while outside the jet age erupted with a fall of poison dust.

Sitting in his velvet cushions, a glass of scotch in his hand and the comfortable elegance of the princess's drawing room about him, he had gone off. 'Jarvey's off again catching flies. You'll have to have your tonsils done if you can't shut the gate.' He wondered what she would have said to see him there. Philomela she would have categorized as 'very à la', Raphael's voice as decidedly 'pound-notish', and called the two Cracknells 'funny old farts with more money than sense'. They were telling some story of their war, at least the princess was, of their driving days together during the blitz and Jarvis had a moment's picture of his father standing in a corner in his ARP helmet with a gasmask at his hip while the two ambulances clanged past and a cone of searchlights traced problems in geometry on the blackboard sky. He must be getting drunk. If the fuzz could see him sitting there they would think he had pulled the biggest con trick of all time.

Philomela caught his eye. 'I think we ought to go to bed,' she said rising. There were cries of disappointment from the others, like threatened children. 'Well, you can all keep Cinderella hours if you like, but Jarvis and I are on active service and we need our beauty sleep.' Obediently he had tossed back his scotch. At the door he paused to look back at the elderly tea party, a little owlish now. The major was definitely looking spryer; Althea quite animated. He followed Philomela upstairs.

'I wonder you have the face,' he said as he put his arms round her. 'Active service!'

Four

'The present is beastly but when I think of the future how good it is! I feel so light, so free; there is a light in the distance. I see freedom.'

'Will someone give us the wire when it's best to do it?' Chuff asked. 'I take it you've got a plant in there as well?'

'It's surprising how many people hate their jobs and yet go on doing them,' said Philomela.

'That's because the only ways off the production line are ones the authorities don't care for.'

'You can always change a job.'

'Yes, but it's only like changing hats really, they're all just lids to keep the rain off and sometimes you can't even afford to do that. It's only when you've got enough not to need another job that you can wait about for the right one. And anyway there aren't many right ones, are there? "Energetic, intelligent young man (or woman come to that) seeks interesting well-paid job with travel, perks, lovely people, easy hours" and gets forty to fifty hours at a workbench in noise and artificial light or dull office for enough money, maybe, for a roof overhead and telly licence. The best things in life are free, my arse.'

'Are you preaching to me, Brother Chuff?'

'No, I'm sorry. I was working off a bit of what coppers call "aggro" in their illiterate way that's robbed us of our proper talk.'

'To answer your first question: yes we will be told. It will be a Sunday when they've disposed of all the live animals in the lairages so that none of them will get hurt.'

'Lairage? What sort of a word is that?'

'It's a euphemism, a cover-up for what you're really saying

like "food-unit" for animal. It's where the animals are penned waiting for the chop.'

'How much do they know? How much do they really feel?'

'Nobody knows. There's a lot of discussion about it of course, and a certain amount of research, but the range of opinion runs from almost nothing to as much as we do.'

'They must feel something or they wouldn't shout when they're hurt. You wouldn't be able to train a dog not to pee all over the place if a clout didn't hurt it.'

'It's hard to tell how much they feel of fear because supposedly they don't know what's happening to them and they can't say.'

'The same's true of humans, of course. I don't suppose all those millions who've been shunted about in railway trucks to be shot or gassed knew for sure. They'd go on hoping but they'd be frightened. It's just instinct to be frightened when you're not in control of yourself. You see men in the nick after a time if they don't become violent start to degenerate, go soft and grey for the same reasons because they're not responsible for their own lives. They're in a state of fright and the only way they can deal with it is by stopping feeling as much as they can. You take an animal that's responsible for its own life like a lion, no say a wild deer, that shows pain and fear if you hunt it but it's not much different from a cow really, not physically. What I mean is you could take a race of humans and breed them up in prison conditions and they wouldn't react quite the same way that outside humans would. You might say they didn't show as much fear or pain as outsiders and you could go on and on doing it for generations until they were as docile as lambs to the slaughter. You're breeding the fear out of them along with all the responsibility and freedom of choice.'

'Does an animal have freedom of choice?'

'A bit if it's wild. It can decide whether to go on sleeping or to go out looking for food. That's about the most basic choice we any of us have. It seems to me that what you take away from an animal if you shut it up is by and large what you take away from a man if you shut him up and that is what it might have been.

'Look how many dolphins for instance must have been killed, taking away what they might have been, and now we find out they're as bright as a waggonload of monkeys and might even be able to talk.

'Me, I'm like everybody else. I never gave it a thought until now, just followed what I'd been brought up to, but once you start to consider, well it doesn't really bear thinking about.'

'Shall I tell you something I like about you, funny Chuff?'

'Yeah, if you think I can stand it.'

'I don't know quite what to call it.'

'I hoped it was me lovely blue eyes.'

'Yes,' Philomela said, 'I think it may be.'

> This little pig went to market
> This little pig stayed at home
> This little pig had roast beef
> And this little pig had none

And the really clever little pig, Jarvis thought, went wee, wee, wee, wee all the way home. They always said pigs' cunts were the nearest to human ones. He'd never been close enough to find out and he didn't think he'd begin now. Necrophilia and bestiality weren't his line of country. Excuse me, may I take a walk in your public gardens? Come to think of it the whole idea of having it off with an animal was a bit strange and yet it was always turning up in the porn mags: shepherd boys and sheep, women with stallions, ladies with their pekes and poodles, cowmen. Not only that, there were all those stories in legends about humans and animals and a lot of people had had animal gods or gods who became animals to get at pretty girls or lads. Which animal would he pick if he was hard pushed? Usually it seemed to be the one closest to you but that could be just because it was available or because you'd got fond of it. The black tom called Peter they'd had once had had the biggest set of equipment anyone had ever seen on a moggy and when you saw him from behind as he was walking, the pair of them moved from side to side like black marbles in a tight silk bag. You could make him toss off easy too. Not that he needed much help. Scratch his belly a little and the little pink hard tongue would be out and perking droplets of cream in a flash. Jarvis used to do it surreptitiously when his mother wasn't looking or he'd watch Peter washing himself to catch the moment when his head went down between his back legs, one flung out for greater ease, and the piece of abrasive lint begin licking, licking at the red bud.

How much enjoyment had Peter got from it? His eyes had seemed glazed and he'd blinked at Jarvis a couple of times after. Even if you said it was just a mechanical reflex so was tossing yourself off and you got relief, if not actual pleasure, from that. Somehow scratching Peter's belly to see if he'd come was different from putting it up a sheep or a pig or letting a dog suck you off if you were a woman. Though now he came to think of it it was probably a difference of degree rather than kind. Probably some people got a kick out of mating their animals if you pushed it far enough back. It was like incest in a way though he couldn't remember that he'd ever fancied Madeleine. He'd looked at her and wondered of course, at what the shoulder straps were holding up through the lemon nylon blouse and just how far he could see up her skirt when she sat down. Not that he wanted to do anything about it but just to snatch a half look. So now he wondered about pigs' cunts. 'You want to know the ins and outs of a mog's arse with your questions.'

Funny he'd never come across anyone inside who'd been done for it. Yet there were people, mainly in country districts though, so maybe that was why he'd never met any. Perhaps they always put them in the hospital wing. The other cons would have made their lives a misery; they were bad enough with ordinary sex cases. But suppose the animal made up to you. Zoo keepers for instance. He could imagine a lady chimp might take quite a shine to someone who fed her and looked after her. Sometimes you saw an alsatian trying to fuck a child. 'Excuse me, my lord, but this bitch wouldn't leave me alone.' After all we're only animals too.

In all our imaginations there was beauty and the beast; King Kong holding the girl in the palm of his hand and wondering where to put it. Like the story of the Red Indian who caught a mermaid and threw her back and when his friend asked him 'Why?' he answered 'How?' That was it: how? How did your mother and father? What did they do to get you when you were just a twinkle in your father's eye? Whose eye had twinkled for him, he wondered. It was hard to think of the old man being a young spark. Maybe his mother had led him on. 'Excuse me, my lord, but this bitch . . .'

With half of our minds we tried to cut ourselves off from them, to pretend we were quite different. Perhaps after all it was a barrier that didn't exist and that was what we were afraid of. Cannibalism that would make it, if we once dropped the barrier or else we should have to admit there was no such thing and all flesh was just . . . grass. We were the same as the wolf and the shark and the tarantula however we tried to dodge out of it. We liked to think of ourselves as cavemen running down mammoths and sabre-toothed tigers, as the pride of lions, but we were closer to chimps ganging up on a helpless, gormless young baboon to tear it to pieces. Chuff remembered a news clipping about an expedition to some dark interior thriving on the boiled monkey served up by the native bearers. Ugh, the home bodies said, but where was the difference between monkey and pig except that monkey looked like human baby and reminded us that the barrier didn't exist? Aborigine mothers killed one of their children and served it to the other so that it would grow big and strong with the lifeblood and doubled spirit. Cannibals gobbled up their enemies for the same reason.

What could or couldn't be done wasn't based on reason but on superstition and habit. Once in a drinking session on prison rotgut they'd asked a gentle Jewboy to explain about eating kosher. The other four had been very reasonable with him and it had been clear that it was just a form of abracadabra to protect him. But it had come to Jarvis in the middle of the discussion, done in the half-dark by a rigged-up pink light, that the same arguments turned against the arguers' own eating habits would have met only the same unreasonable replies. Filthy foreigners ate frogs' legs.

Jarvis enjoyed raw flesh. He stole the steak and kidney from the pile waiting at his mother's elbow while she lined the pudding basin with a linenfold of dough. Once he'd eaten raw herring to prove he could only to learn when he grew up that smoked salmon was a recognized delicacy. Best of all meat he liked offal: stuffed hearts, kidneys, liver, brains. The parson's nose was as sweet as a nut his mother said and they took turns for it. But he drew the line at lights, which only went to show

how unreasoning it all was since the Germans, who after all were our cousins, ate great piles of them.

It was a ritual he loved to watch. When his mother skinned and prepared a rabbit the lights and windpipe were dropped for the cat rubbing against the table leg: the heart cut from them carefully cleaned of its solid black blood and placed in the salt water with the liver and kidneys. His mother's fingers swollen with cold water were surgeon delicate as she skinned the knobby kidneys of their cellophane membrane. 'Is Peter's skin like that Mum?' Jarvis asked as his mother pulled it off like a tight glove, wrenching the slim wrists through to leave four furry paws on the naked body. Could you feel yourself moving inside it like we could in our clothes? 'That's how they carry their kittens by the scruff of the neck.' Then she would take the kitchen knife and the hammer and cleave the small skull neatly in two from back to front so there could be no fighting over brains and tongue.

He remembered it without squeamishness, as he sometimes thought of donating his body to the hospital and the uses they might put it to. The preparation had been like a laying-out and the rabbit was given honourable burial first in the pot and then in their bellies. Pretty in life, it was clean and dignified in death. Would humans be the same or would they be as rancid and unpalatable as they were often unlovely alive? Like pork perhaps? He had read somewhere that human ate like pig. Maybe that was why Moses forbade it. Maybe he'd read about pigs' cunts too or been tempted in the desert.

This little pig ate roast beef, and what about the one Tom ran off with? It could have been a fate worse than death. If so it was harshly punished while Tom, whose fault it all was, got merely a walloping. Sometimes the rabbit had been pitted with blue holes and his mother had had to cut the small pellets of buckshot out of the flesh, clucking over the spoiling and the possibility that it mightn't be killed outright but drag itself about wounded for days. 'You can tell if it dies in pain. The meat's dark and acidy.' He thought now this must have been a bit of a fairy story told them both to prove that most of the time it was all right. It was the dying not the corpse that brought you up short. The knife gritted through the jerking eel-spines behind the gills as if you were nipping through expanding rod with the pinchers and it was only later you realized you had clipped off life. The tail end threshed about like a stretched man but it was the loosening of the strung wires that held the puppet together, not a last protest of quenched life force. Life was frail and easily broken. What you could never put back you had to pretend didn't matter. Its vulnerability and temporariness could make it seem worthless beside the gaping black shark mouth that would gulp it down. Lew Ayres stretched out his hand to the butterfly and fell back. The city domes blazed and rang while the wolves and the forest snapped black at the rocketing sledge.

'Looks like a picture palace,' Jarvis said as they drove past the white-tiled façade with its decorations of marble palm trees dipping lapis lazuli fronds over the doorway to Tutankhamun's tomb. 'Cleopatra'll come down those steps in a minute with a cast of thousands all in towels and slave bangles.'

'Sometimes,' Philomela said, 'I wonder if you spent most of your childhood in the cinema.'

'Course I did. Tuesdays and Thursdays, Saturday morning and Sunday afternoon. "Will you take us in, lady?" and round the back through the exit when you couldn't afford a ticket. I bet you never saw Don Winslow and the Scorpion. It was a serial that only ran on Saturday mornings.' As usual before a job he felt high and clear-headed at the same time.

'That's only the front,' said Philomela, 'the back view's very different.'

'And that's our view.' Jarvis turned down a side street at right-angles to the De Mille frontage, drove for same way along a black brick wall and turned again round the block, cruising slowly along the fencing wall at the back, with its sharp battlements of broken bottle catching occasional dull gleams from the street lightning.

For a moment it seemed to Jarvis that they were driving in time as well as space as the streets of his childhood grew in identikit pattern around him, the terraces ranking the street in the factory precision of two-storey artisan dwellings, the corner shop smelling of mice and bacon where sugar and soda were done up in blue cartridge bags and vinegar was sold loose, the lamps with their convenient bar for throwing a rope over, the immortal blackened privet between the front room curtains and the pavement.

The curtain wall was pierced in the middle by heavy double wooden doors, with a pedestrian door to the right. 'No portcullis?' Jarvis asked.

'It'd be on the inside to keep things in rather than people out.'

'That little door looks a cinch. I'll open it up as an emergency exit. Night watchman?' He checked.

'Round the front in the office block. He'll stay there until he phones the fire brigade.'

'I bet it don't half pong in the summer and when they're boiling up.' He could imagine the local comments on the doorsteps as the fronts were swept of grit and blown papers in the morning. 'Better get your clothes in dear they've got the pot on.''His mates at work'd think he'd pooped his pants if I was to leave them out to dry in that stink.'

Beyond the wall a chimney rose like a central keep. 'It's bloody enormous,' Chuff said as they drove on round the perimeter.

'There used to be a dog patrol but they got rid of that after complaints about the risk to children. Now there's just the alarm system to the offices . . .'

'The picture palace?' They were telling each other things they had already rehearsed, for comfort.

'That's right, but luckily the factory and slaughterhouse aren't wired. It would be too complicated.'

'I noticed on the plan. There are lots of outbuildings and entrances.' They turned for the last time. Here the wall was backed by a piece of waste land with trees and brambles, mainly the playground of children and dogs.

For this jaunt they had a Triumph Spitfire with new number-plates. Jarvis wore a sporty cap; Philomela a head-scarf though they had kept the hood on. Among the narrow streets Jarvis had felt his disguise an obscure betrayal, knowing what the reactions of passers-by would be. But there had been no one to pass judgement. The pubs were closed; the drinkers safely home. Even the small oblong tanks where the underwater television lives played on hour after hour, had shrunk to a point of white light in the black pool and then to nothing but darkness.

A long-disused door was set into the wall. Chuff knew that its lock and hinges had been oiled and that it was ready to give at a touch. He took a deep breath as they left the safety of the car and put an arm round Philomela. They dawdled towards the door through the sooty grass and scrub. Keeping a smart lookout, Jarvis pushed Philomela's back against the door and leaned against her, his arms round her soft body, a hand feeling for the lock.

Philomela put her mouth to his ear and bit gently. 'You'd better hurry,' she said. 'I don't know how much of this I can stand.' The key turned with a small click.

'We're in,' said Jarvis, unwilling to let her go. With a last look round he pressed firmly against the door which scraped open. Once they were through he set it back innocently in place.

The buildings were very black against the sky. Philomela switched on a pencil torch for a moment and flickered it across their path in case a workman had left a drum or barrow they could bang into.

'Up the ramp,' Chuff whispered. They crossed the concrete yard to the entrance where the lorries would back up and drop their tailboards to let the animals flock through into the building. Jarvis dealt with the padlock and chain. 'Stay there.' Taking out his own torch he went back to unlock the little door in the back wall. 'In we go.' They only needed to open one half of the double door enough to let them slip through. Philomela's torch pencilled in the dark interior, smelling mutedly of hay and animal bodies with an overtone of coal-tar disinfectant.

'Lairages to the left. Engine house straight ahead.' In there they found the paraffin and cotton waste they needed. Carrying these they let themselves through the animal pens, where they would be rested to recover from their journey for a day or more before slaughter, and up the ramp that ended in a sliding door Jarvis pushed open. 'Slaughter hall.'

'Sheep slaughter hall,' Philomela corrected quietly. Mutton pies, lambs' tongues, saddle, shoulder, leg and chop. It was funny, Jarvis thought, how many buildings looked like nicks, as if men had to go on repeating the same old pattern, as if they'd got the needle stuck and couldn't push on to the next bit and make sense of the tune. Everywhere there were nicks: schools, hospitals, asylums, factories and now this. Perhaps it was the pens made him think so or the doors shutting one bit from another so those waiting below couldn't see or smell what was coming, like the wardrobe in the old condemned peter that moved aside to let you see the last door you'd go through.

Overhead was a system of metal rails with hoists, hooks and chains. The walls were white and smooth. At one end stood the metal box of the stunning pen. Chuff led the way through the bleeding passage where the butcher's shop odour of blood and carcase was strongest although there was no more sign of them than in an empty operating theatre. The very emptiness gave the rooms a brooding watchfulness and it was hard not to break into a trot.

Beyond the slaughter hall was the cooling room. Chuff pushed open the door, paused a moment and then went in. White carcases hung in neat railed rows in the gloom, the torch shining wetly on the bloomed fat of sheep, bloodily on the beef. 'We'll do the cold store first and work our way back,' Chuff said to break the quiet.

'Better to stick to the plan,' Philomela answered. 'You get on with the pigs, I'll do the cold store as we arranged. I'll meet you back in here.' She moved firmly towards the refrigerated room where tonight the current would be switched off and the door held back. Chuff turned reluctantly to the pigs' cooling room. He had to pass through the cattle-dressing section among the gigantic hoists and benches, past the electric bonesaw to the pig department and as he went it seemed as if he was escaping again, as if the weeks in between were a dream of the night before and he was alone creeping towards the library. How was Philomela feeling, he wondered, and took comfort just from the thought of her.

The white walls and gleaming metal seemed endless in their repetition. He had brought a can of paraffin with him, leaving one behind and it began to hang deadweight from his hand. The carcases of the pigs when he finally reached them were strung like the sheep and cattle but still with their heads, moulded in pink wax after the scalding tank and dehairing machine, the parody of living flesh in the set cold corpse making them appear like pink sugar mice, as if they had never lived.

> 'This little pig went to market
> This little pig didn't stay home
> This little pig became roast pork . . .'

Jarvis muttered as he douched the smooth skins with paraffin until it ran down their faces in oily tears and dripped from their noses and ears. Then he passed quickly among the rows lighting them here and there like long candles that began to flame and splutter at once as the tongues licked up the hides. Crackling, trotters, brawn and bacon, loin, belly, hand, spring, sausages and pies sizzled and melted while Chuff stood devilish among them with his cotton waste flambeau. He must hurry back. Philomela would be waiting.

Now he ran through the concrete halls, found the can he had left, but no Philomela, and began to slosh fuel over the hanging beef and lamb. There had been a film, but he couldn't quite pin it down, of protection rackets in Chicago among the stock yards that nagged at the back of his mind as if he had done all this somewhere before. The can was empty. Where was Philomela? Perhaps he should give her a hand. He moved towards the cold store with the paraffin reek around overpowering the smells of meat and blood. One half side of beef he passed looked dark and bruised in the torchlight. Cagmag, his mother would have called it, dark as horsemeat and as tough. He stepped through the passage to the heavy door of the cold store. It was shut.

For nearly five seconds he was poleaxed; his mind refused to register or understand. The door should have been opened. He reached out his gloved hand and yanked on the heavy metal handle. The door stayed shut. At once he let the handle drop, turned and ran through into the cattle-dressing hall and down towards the stunning pens, the torch casting about as he ran, raking the room for something he could use as a lever. On a table he saw what looked like a pistol and snatched it up. Perhaps he could shoot the door down. Philomela must be inside. In a rack he saw a collection of cleavers and axes, picked the longest and narrowest he could find and ran back to the door. Slipping the blade under the handle he levered up, controlling the force he put on for fear of snapping the metal arm right off.

It gave suddenly, the door swung open and Philomela tumbled out in a belch of smoke and heat, coughing in the stench of roasting flesh. She was alive and still conscious and untouched by the flames flowering behind her. With one arm round her shoulders he helped her out into the dressing hall. 'Stay here. Won't be a minute.' Jarvis ran back into the cooling room. The flames from the cold-store oven would reach out into the passage but perhaps not far enough. He lit bonfires in a few carcases and laid a trail of paraffin to the remaining tin.

Philomela was recovering rapidly. Jarvis led her down the ramp and past the pens to the back door which he opened enough for them to slip through into the cold fresh air where they stood a moment taking deep breaths. He crossed the yard to the little door, drew it carefully towards him and looked out into the street. There was no one about. The eyes in the windows opposite were blank. The torch flicked quickly on-off in signal for her to join him.

'Lean on me. Pretend you're fond of me.'

'I am,' she said, taking his arm. 'I'm all right now. It was fright and the smoke.'

'I'd have gone bloody berserk shut in there.'

They sauntered as if they were out for an evening stroll. 'The door must have slammed behind me and it can't be opened from the inside of course. I just sat as close to it as I could and prayed you'd come to look for me.'

'The bleeding door jammed, that was why I was so long. The sodding thing wouldn't open.' They turned the corner by the piece of waste ground. 'Look,' said Chuff. Behind the windows of the first floor a pink glow was spreading and deepening like a pool of split blood. 'When does the night watchman ring the fire brigade?'

'He'll look up on his next round if he doesn't see anything before.' They got into the car. Jarvis wound down the window. With a dull whump a banner of flame streamed suddenly from a smashed window and then was withdrawn.

'That's the paraffin can,' Jarvis said. 'He'd better ring them now.'

'He's quite safe. The office is cut off from the factory, remember, and there's still the factory between.' Philomela wound down her window. 'My whole body smells of burning fat.' She opened her handbag, took out a phial of scent and filled the car with its smell.

'Nobody was to get hurt, we said, and you could have been killed in there, asphyxiated or worse. If I couldn't have got that fucking door open . . .'

'But you did. I knew you would. Listen.'

Far off sounded the heralding clang of a fire engine. By now, Chuff thought, faces would be pressed to bedroom windows in the street behind.

'Drive round to the front and let's watch for a while,' Philomela said.

'Isn't that a bit risky?'

'So risky no one would think of it.'

They pulled into the main road, beating the fire engine by seconds. Other cars were drawing up at a distance to watch the excitement. 'There's nothing like a good blaze to bring the bugs out of the woodwork,' Chuff said. Two more fire tenders drew up, together with a control van and a police car. The crowd on the pavement thickened.

'That's the night watchman,' said Philomela. A little man had come forward and was talking to the police and senior fire officer.

'Looks like an old-style bookie's runner. Is he a cherub?'

'No. He was just paid to keep out of harm's way.'

'The cherub was someone else?'

She nodded. 'Cherubs don't get paid. In a big place like this there's lots of coming and going among the work force. It's easy to slip people in as casuals.'

The sky behind the temple deepened its usual city glow. 'She's really going now. We couldn't have done better if we'd rubbed two boy scouts together.' Two fire engines and the control car set off down the sidestreet. 'I hope those firemen don't go in for any fancy stuff over an empty building but just let the bugger burn.' More police cars were arriving.

Philomela yawned. 'Take me home, Chuff, please. I'm suddenly terribly tired.'

They left the Triumph in the Chelsea back street behind the King's Road where they had parked their own. In the morning, Chuff supposed, the owner, who was probably a wealthy cherub, would change back the plates and replace his resident's permit. If he had really wanted to know, Chuff could probably have tracked him down. He hoped the cherub wouldn't settle for a lie-in or have forgotten to set his alarm. At the least it would mean a fine. At the worst he might set a whole train going that would blow up in their faces. Jarvis decided to keep that thought to himself. Philomela, when he took a sideways glance, was looking a bit peaky, her head leaning against the window, eyes closed. He cleared his throat. 'You all right?'

'Just a little tired, I think.'

Jarvis stepped on the pedal with an eye on the speedometer and another on the driving mirror for anything coming up fast behind and flashing a blue light. If she admitted to not feeling too special it probably meant delayed shock was catching up on her. Thank Christ for cars. God knows how people managed when they had to trundle through the countryside for miles on horseback.

The princess and Raphael were waiting up for them. Chuff suspected that she always did unless Philomela rang her. As they pulled up outside the lighted window Philomela said, 'Don't tell Aunt Lottie about my getting shut in. She'd only worry.'

'If you say so. It could have happened to anybody, you know that, don't you?'

'You mean it wasn't because I'm an amateur and a woman.'

'That's right. It could just as well have been me in there and you getting me out.'

She put a hand on his and it came to Chuff that no one had ever done that to him before. He might have had leprosy for all any bird had ever wanted to touch his hand. 'You're very nice to me, Chuff.'

Jarvis watched her anxiously while they told a watered-down

version of the night's antics. Finally he stood up, initiating the move upstairs. Philomela's face was smudged with tiredness as well as smoke and Jarvis felt the gravel beginning to turn behind his own eyelids. 'No more jobs for a few days,' he said at the top of the stairs. 'If the major's got anything else lined up it'll have to wait.'

As he turned to close the door of his pink bedroom he felt something heavy swing against it in his jacket pocket. It was the gun he had picked up earlier that evening. Now that he had time to examine it properly he could see it was like no gun he had ever handled before or even seen in the manual of small arms. Jarvis put it in a drawer under the pyjamas he had never used. He would ask Philomela about it. Perhaps she would know what it was. She seemed to know everything else.

A sound outside made him cross to the window and open it. A faint overspill of light seemed to be coming from the direction of the chapel. For a moment he wasn't sure and then unmistakably he heard the familiar chorus picking up from the verse.

> 'All things bright and beautiful,
> All creatures great and small;
> All things wise and wonderful,
> The Lord God made them all.'

Aunt Lottie was celebrating their latest success. Jarvis grinned and closed the window.

Seriously he wondered if he was going off his rocker. In the morning Philomela hadn't come down to breakfast. He had gone up and knocked on her door and, when she had called him in, found her, pale and sweaty, her tousled hair giving her face a waif's look against the pillow. His belly seemed to go right through his boots.

'It's all right,' she said. 'I just feel a bit grotty. I'll have an aspirin and sleep for a while.'

Now he was down at the bottom of the park among the leaves and the rooks when he would much rather have been straddled across her door like the miserable hound he felt. The sun and the warm, shining grass winked mockingly at him. The white glare across the park hurt his eyes and made the ground at his feet tilt. From here he could see the sun catch her window and be thrown back at him. Insects twittered and buzzed in the grass. Overhead the rooks argy-bargied among themselves. 'It's all right for you lot,' he said.

He wanted to throw himself down on the turf and thump the unyielding ground except that he might have been seen from the house. All because some bird was lying ill down there he wanted to swear and shout and smash things. He must be going right round the twist. Where was Jarvis Chuff, escapee, hard case? The shell had a crack in it where a soft kernel had put out a painful shoot. He felt like a pea grown in a jam jar in damp blotting paper. His body was the jam jar and the first shoot grew white with jagged sucking rootlets down into his guts while the other shot up his spinal column and filled his brainbox with leaves and flowers, flyaway sweet-pea blooms that would open their frail pastel wings and take off out of his eyes. The strange pain down in the pit of his stomach must be the roots taking hold.

Only once before had he ever felt like it and that was when he had come home one day to find his mother lying on the floor in the living room in a puddle of her own blood. 'I'm sorry, Jarvey,' she said, 'to be a nuisance,' and died on him, becoming part of a statistic: those who die from falls in their own home. She had been up the ladder sweeping the ceiling with a duster on a broom. 'Bloody fidget-arse,' he'd said in the dialogues he carried on with her in his head for weeks after, 'you couldn't let well alone could you? Always had to be at something, didn't you?' It was one of these that had engaged him in the middle of his next job and made him careless, costing him five years while he contemplated the bricks and the dialogue sank to a monologue where he couldn't hear her voice any more, just his own accusations. Only when he stopped accusing her did the voice come back, but from an earlier childhood time, strong and quick to tease him.

A strange drumming noise brought him back. Beyond the line of trees was a small stream, a piece of flat meadow spiked with rushes and a low hedge. As he looked up a flying shape sailed over the hedge, landed with a slight skid and cantered towards him: Delilah with Althea atop, both breathing heavily. Althea walked the horse over to him and dismounted. 'She will do it, you know. As soon as she sees that hedge she's away. I've tried to make her go round but if she once takes off there's no stopping her.'

'How's the major?' Chuff asked politely.

'Oh he's fine. And all the rest of the menagerie. I came to see Philly. Lottie said on the phone she wasn't too good.'

'Got rather a shake-up yesterday, I expect,' said Jarvis coolly. 'It was a bit hairy in there.'

'She wouldn't have liked it anyway. Soft as butter that girl, for all she seems so composed. The place would have upset her.'

'You think so?' Jarvis was more concerned to keep the conversation on the topic of Philomela than what the old duck might think.

'Definitely. Known her for years. One evening we were having dinner. She was home for the holidays and Lottie had let her stay up. Ferdinand was still alive and her father too but he was away somewhere. Suddenly she came out with it. "Do I have to go on eating dead animals at school?" Very calmly. "Of course not," Lottie said. "That's all right then." And we never heard any more about it. What I mean is, a lot more goes on inside than she lets show.'

Jarvis tucked that one away for later, together with the pleasure this glimpse of her childhood gave him. He felt pretty much soft as butter inside himself, butter put in front of the fire in the dish to warm in winter and forgotten till it began to run to golden oil, with an icing of salty scum, that would harden to near transparency if you took it away from the heat.

'I'd better get along,' said Althea. 'You coming?' Jarvis shook his head. 'Look after her,' Althea said gruffly. 'She would do it, you know. Obstinate as this one,' she patted the horse's neck.

'I do try,' said Chuff.

*

'The next one should be quite simple,' the major had said, 'in fact really what one might call a joyride,' and he had laughed rustily.

'What is it then?' Chuff asked suspiciously.

'Philomela will tell you.'

She was up and about the next day but a bit wan still, Jarvis thought. His dream had come back, only this time the city was burning and he knew Philomela was inside the closed gates. He lay awake after, looking at the lead-grey squares of window and wondered if his nerve was going and how many more jobs they would have to do. Chuff's law said the more you did, the higher the likelihood of getting caught or hurt and it also said that if you weren't high and cool as you went in then ditto Brother Smuts on your chances of coming out. Now he wanted to come through and that in itself was wrong. It was only when you didn't care that you could be perfectly clear and single-minded. And he cared so much it hurt and amazed him. This must be how foxes felt with all the world on their tail and nothing in their bodies but the chemicals combusting for survival.

'Aunt Lottie insists on coming too for the first part,' Philomela said. 'The idea is to drop thousands of leaflets on London, setting out the aims of the group. First they have to be collected and she wants to come with us. She says she'd be good cover.'

'Where are they?'

'In the crypt of a church in Suffolk.'

'How the hell did they get there?'

'They're printed on a hand-press by a man who used to run a poetry magazine in Lincolnshire until the Arts Council stopped his grant.'

'Won't they be traceable?'

'Not really. You see the type, which is the really traceable thing, is an old one that's been used for years by different underground organizations. It printed IRA material in the twenties and leaflets for the Jarrow march. Then it was used for Spanish republican news sheets. During the war the Free French had it. When the war ended Spies for Peace took it over for a while until it passed to the Grow Up and Love groups. It'll drop out of sight until someone needs it. So it can't ever be traced to the printer.'

'But why the crypt?'

'Parish magazines of course. We have to pick them up, take them to a private airfield and help with the drop.'

'What do we carry them in?'

'Aunt Lottie thought perhaps a coffin.'

'It's been done.'

'What about a tall horsebox with a small horse? The leaflets could be stacked in the bottom.'

'Suppose it watered them for you?'

'Polythene bags. We could borrow Delilah.'

'What I don't see is why she should go to church.'

'She hasn't been well. It's for the laying on of hands.'

'Faith-healing?' Philomela nodded. 'But they don't do that to animals. Do they?'

'St Francis did. And now the archbishop has been forced to admit they might have souls . . .'

'You don't believe all that do you?' Jarvis worried.

'No, but if other people want to, I don't mind.'

'You mean Aunt Lottie?'

'That's right.'

'Suppose the vicar won't play?'

'Then we'll get Raphael to perform the ceremony. But I'm sure he won't mind.'

'Oh gawd,' said Chuff, 'bless this horse.'

'The vicar's delighted to oblige,' Philomela said that evening when they were having their after-dinnger noggin.

'You know he'd do anything for you,' said the princess. Chuff felt both sets of short hairs prickle.

'When I was seventeen he wanted to marry me,' Philomela explained. 'It was all very who's-for-tennis and strawberries on the lawn.' She smiled with blatant sexiness at Jarvis. 'I don't think I'd have made a good vicar's wife, do you?'

'He'll lay on a little service and encourage the local children and pensioners to bring their pets. I can lead Delilah in, she's always very good with me, while Philomela loads the leaflets,' the princess went on.

'What do I do?' Jarvis asked.

'You won't be there,' said Philomela. 'You'll come straight to the airfield that night.'

'Nothing doing. I'm coming with you.'

'It was Philomela's idea,' said the princess hastily.

'Oh, was it? Well it's not on, see.'

'It'll be daylight. Suppose we were stopped or someone recognized you?'

'We'll have to see they don't then. You haven't worried about that before. Besides if you have to load all that stuff alone you'll be worn out and after . . .' He was going to spill the lot when Philomela's eyes warned him. '. . . after being not well,' he ended half-heartedly.

'We'll discuss it later,' Philomela said.

'Now what's it all about?' Jarvis asked as she shut the door of her room behind them.

'I just don't want you getting caught. What's wrong with that?'

'Look,' he said, 'you took this on because you didn't want the old dears hurt and you got me in for the same reason. Now you want to protect me as well. What are you going to do? Spring someone else so I don't get hurt. You can't do it. I'm part of the risk.'

'It's so unfair. We got you into this and you're the one who's got the most to lose.'

'Yes,' he said, 'I have got the most to lose but only now because you gave it to me. I've been half dead up till now. Now I don't want to go inside ever again and I'm going to do everything I bloody well can to stay out but that doesn't involve your doing my share of the work. I'd be worried sick hanging around waiting for you and wondering what was going on and if you're all right. So set your mind to work on how we can tart me up so me own mother wouldn't know me. Where you go I go, as the man said.'

'I think,' said Philomela, 'it was probably a woman.'

'I suppose we could always dress me up like Widow Twanky, but then you look so bloody daft when you're caught.'

*

Chuff eased the car out on to the road feeling the un-accustomed drag of the loosebox behind. In the rear mirror he could see the princess and, if he shifted a bit to one side, Philomela on the back seat. They had decided on a stable-boy's rig for him, with dark hair and moustache so that he looked a real gippo or like Don Ameche in *The Three Musketeers*. 'But later,' Philomela said, 'we'll think of something better.'

Maybe he should have been a stable-lad, he thought, as they unwound their cross-country route. You could be anything, given the right set of clothes. The pity of it was that most people didn't get the chance to be anything else once they were set in a certain way. We were all allotted our colours like the layers in a liquorice allsort and if you wanted to be orange or brown when you were pink that was too bad. Once you grew up you were supposed to stop all that, kids' games of pretend, and get down to reality. What was so special about reality and how was it more real than what you could be? The nick was real enough when you were inside but now it seemed almost an invention he had thought up on a wet afternoon to torment himself with. This was real: that his name was Gabriel, dark-haired, black-tashed diddicai Gabriel who laid the missus when he was lucky and was driving her now through sharp green leaves where birds hopped and sopranoed. The sun flashed bright messages from the shiny bonnet and water dazzle flick-ered in the road ahead. A pheasant in the safety of the close season peacocked along the plush veridian verge.

'So come all you gallant poachers and listen to my song,
It is a piece of good advice although it is not long;
Lay down your gun and snare, to you I do speak plain,
If you knew the sorrows we endure you ne'er would hunt again.'

Jarvis sang in his head. The church was cobbled with flints. Its spire rose out of rich deep foliage beyond pinkwashed cottages. They had by-passed Cambridge and crossed the county bound-ary at Prickwillow. 'I don't believe it,' Chuff said and then hoped the princess hadn't heard.

'I suppose I shall have to meet Ruskin,' Philomela said.

'I'm afraid so.'

'But I don't think he should meet Jarvis. He might have an

attack of Anglican conscience some time and it's better if he can honestly say he's never seen him.'

They left Jarvis in the car and went through a wooden gate to the vicarage. Ten minutes later Philomela was back. 'Aunt Lottie is having lunch with Ruskin. We can take Delilah round to a field at the back of the churchyard. The parcels will have to be brought up out of the crypt and through the churchyard.'

'I'll do that while the service is going on.'

The horse seemed pleased to be out of its box. It tossed its head and snorted. Chuff was afraid that it might decide to take off but Philomela talked soothingly as she tethered it to the gatepost on a long rein and it soon put down its head and began to crop the grass. 'What about some grubstakes for us?'

'There's the village pub.'

'If you won't mind being seen with a gippo and if they'll let me in.'

'What's good enough for Lady Chatterley . . .'

'I thought he was a gamekeeper.'

'I'd rather have a gippo,' she said and put her arm through his.

The service began at three. The princess and Philomela led Delilah away and Chuff got down to loading the packs of leaflets under the false bottom of the loosebox. The churchyard drowsed under the acid shade of yew trees as Jarvis sweated gently. From time to time there was a muffled sound of organ and straining voices. The birds were taking a siesta but insects buzzed among the lopsided headstones or sunned themselves briefly on the coffin-shaped tombs. At last the packets were stowed. Jarvis cuffed the sweat from his face with the back of his hand then checked that his moustache hadn't run. He would give a quick eye inside the church to see how they were coming along.

There seemed to be some sort of procession: people and animals going up to the altar steps together where the vicar, he supposed it must be Ruskin, with a fold of pink chin dewlapping his dog-collar Chuff was pleased to see, put one hand on the animal and lifted the other, his lips moving in blessing. The princess had been right about the pensioners and the kids. There were old girls with budgies in cages, an old boy with an ageing black mongrel, children with mice, rabbits, hamsters; a huge tabby lay docile in a mum's arms; a boy led a goat, another had a goldfish in a bowl. Delilah was the only horse. When her turn came the princess led her up and she sank to her haunches and lifted her hoof while lowering her head.

Then the organ struck up again and Jarvis could hear Lottie Shoe's voice lifted above all the others. Philomela stared straight ahead but the princess's face shone with the dedication of a television choirboy. Chuff found himself wanting to sing too though he didn't believe a word of it. Some reflex from assembly at Old Town Junior worked at the muscles in his throat and it was all he could do not to join in.

> 'All creatures of our God and King
> Lift up your voice and with us sing.
> Thou burning sun with golden beam
> Thou silver moon with softer gleam.
> O-oh praise him . . .'

Chuff shut in the quavering voices and went back to the car. A sudden burst of organ voluntary told him they were coming out. In a few minutes Philomela appeared leading the horse with the princess bringing up the rear.

'I did enjoy that. Let me have her, dear. Now Delilah, we'll just take a couple of turns and I want you to be good.' Dutifully on the first turn Delilah let fall a steaming yellow cascade and on the second a generous helping of dung cakes.

'It's a shame to waste it. My mother would have been out the front door in a flash with the coal shovel and bucket to feed the tomatoes. The coalman's horse didn't dare drop it anywhere except outside our house.' He had never before known whether to be ashamed of her or proud.

'At least it should keep the leaflets dry.'

'Don't worry, I wrapped them up well.'

'You're sure you're not to tired to drive?'

'It'd look bloody funny me sitting in the back. You can take a turn when we're on our way home.'

Althea met them at the airfield in a Land-Rover. She had brought food for Delilah and cosseted her with a sugar lump.

A few private singleseaters perched about the grass like gaudy-winged insects ready for flight. There were a couple of large hangars and a small office block. A middle-aged man in overalls came out of the block to meet them. Althea's Land-Rover was parked outside. She set about taking out Delilah at once.

'Chugger,' the princess called delighted and trotted to meet the stocky overalled figure. Chuff saw them kiss each other affectionately, the princess's hair even whiter against his brick-tanned face.

'Lottie, you look bang on as ever.'

'It's terribly good of you, Chug, to do this for us.'

'Wouldn't miss it for worlds. Don't know what it's all about, don't care. Just want a chance to take the old kite up. Show 'em, eh, there's life in us yet and we can still fly the pants off the jet set.'

'Chug, you know Philomela, and this is Gabriel.' He thinks I'm a bounder, Chuff thought as he shook hands.

'Know anything about aircraft?'

'Sorry, I was army.'

'Brown job. Oh well, you've only got to push the stuff out.'

'I'm coming too,' Philomela put in.

'Touch of the Amy Johnson's. It's a good job we're not superstitious like the navy. No doubt you'd give us a bit of stick from Women's Lib if we were. Now where's the load?'

'In there,' Jarvis nodded towards the loosebox.

'Better drive her into the hangar. Thought I'd keep the old girl out of sight till we were ready to go.'

'Do you come here often?' Chuff asked as they climbed back into the car. Chugger was flagging them down towards the second hangar with closed doors.

'What do you mean?'

'To entertain the troops. Can I have the first foxtrot even though I'm only a brown job?'

'Puritan. I like you.'

'Jesus, what the hell's that?'

'I think, but I could be wrong, it's a Lancaster.' Chugger had pushed back one of the double doors and they had driven into the gloom to draw up beside a large cumbersome aircraft that squatted on the floor, a recalcitrant and heavily pregnant queen bee.

'Do you think it'll go?'

'If he remembers to wind up the elastic.'

'Isn't she marvellous?' Chugger said as they bent to look at the dark underbelly.

'What is it?'

'A Lanc, a real live Lanc from the days when men were men and women were women and aircraft were aircraft, not flying bedsteads or space modules.'

'Will it still go?'

'Been working on her for a week. Usually she's slung up there.' He waved his hands towards the roof. 'We'll soon find out. Take off 0100 hours. Better unload your stuff. I rather think Lottie wants to get going.'

Althea was to drive the princess and Delilah back, leaving Jarvis and Philomela the white Rover. Delilah was backed into her caravan. The princess waved. Althea had brought a coat of imitation black Persian lamb to keep the cold from Lottie in the open wagon. From a lengthening distance they looked like two English lady explorers setting off for some unknown steppe. The princess had tied down her hat with a chiffon scarf. Althea wore a salt and pepper Henry Heath.

'There's hours before kick off,' Chuff said. 'I don't fancy sticking about here. Let's go into the nearest town.'

'What would we do there?'

'We could have some proper supper and go to the pictures. Who knows they might even be showing *The Way To The Stars*.'

It was a strange experience to sit next to Philomela in the dark. He might have been fourteen again and dating his first bird except that he'd never felt like this. The film wasn't a mucher but when they came to the bedroom stuff he found himself aching for it to be them. He glanced sideways at Philomela's profile and wondered if it was making her randy too, though it was always said pictures didn't steam birds up. Mysteries they were. He imagined her fourteen and knocking about with different blokes. Perhaps there hadn't been any chance and she'd had to wait till she was left school and going round the world on her tod. He'd been a lucky sod who'd had her first.

Chuff bet the silly bastard didn't know how lucky neither. But he was luckier because he was sitting here with her now and could feel, through his arm pressed against hers on the rest between them, the rise and fall of her breasts as she breathed. The word made him go cold inside and rear up. Tits and bristols were all right for calendar cheesecake and barrack room chat with the boys, but when you were really stuck on a bird you needed something else. 'Boos' his mother had called it; short for bosom, he thought. But that had a matronly sound, and boobs were mid-Atlantic and as appetizing as cold slabs of rice pudding with knobs on. To his own surprise he put out a hand and took hers.

'That was a load of old cobblers.'

'I'm sorry,' she said, as if she were somehow responsible.

'I said we should go. Anyhow I don't mean I didn't enjoy it.'

By the time they got back to the airfield it was nearly half past eleven. 'Listen,' he said. 'There's no call for you to come up in that old crate. I can unload the stuff.'

'I'm coming,' Philomela said firmly, 'so you can give up trying now.'

Chugger met them with another middle-aged man in overalls whom he introduced as 'Flight'. They both wore striped cravats tucked into the neck of their white boilersuit tops. The Lancaster had been moved out on to the runway.

'Do we get parachutes?' asked Chuff.

'Christ, no. Where we're going you'd only end up down a chimney like Santa Claus. Not frightened are you? Dead reliable these old things. Nothing to go wrong, you see.'

'Nor there wasn't with a matchstick and a rubber band but they didn't go far.'

'Anyway you'd better get your bumpf stowed. I'll show you where to shove it out.' They scrambled up after him into the strangely smelling interior. Inside it looked even more unstable with all the ribs showing. 'That's the window chute. We used to chuck laminated foil out of it to muck up their radar. Use that.'

'Ta very much.'

Chuff and Philomela took turns at passing the packs up until they were all on board. 'Right now, you two get yourselves comfortable. We'll warm up for a bit.' A tremendous roar shook the frame then settled to a continuous ear-numbing vibration. Jarvis could hear the two in front shouting a series of checks back and forth between them. The smell and the spinebreaker ridges at his back reminded him of troop transports he'd flown in. Come to think of it, he'd never been up in a civilian plane. He strained forward to watch but it was mainly the backs of two heads and unidentifiable arm movements.

'Ready for take-off.'

The bile rose in the back of Chuff's throat as the heavy machine began its run up. He felt the tail lift, the ungainly bird straining to be off. This was it. He looked across at Philomela and grinned. Well, if he had to go, and he did some time, it was a better way than most. Flight was shouting speeds. 'Ninety, a hundred, a hundred and ten, a hundred and twenty.' And suddenly Chuff knew the ground was gone, the aircraft droning steeply like an old man climbing a ladder.

'Wheels up.' He felt them clunk into place below him.

'Flaps.'

'Flaps coming in by degrees. Ten, ten, ten, thirty.'

Surely they were safe now, unless all four bloody engines packed it in together. There was the getting down again but they needn't worry about that just now. They had levelled out. At least that was how Jarvis understood the loss of the sensation that he was being dragged back through the tail.

Chugger left his seat and came back to join them. 'I've put her on George.'

'How's she doing?'

'Piece of cake.' He made a suggestive circle of his forefinger and thumb. Obviously he was thoroughly enjoying himself. 'Marvellous chance. Can't afford to take her up you see. Cost us four hundred gallons just to get this far. Cost dear old Lottie, rather, and it's a hundred per cent stuff. Goes like a bomb still. When do you want to start chucking out?'

'Do we go over Reading?'

'Can do.'

'Right, some there. Then as much of London as you can manage.'

'Have to watch out for the Heathrow flight paths. I'll come down to two thousand so you get a good scatter.'

'How fast are we going?'

'About a hundred and eighty.' Chuff thought of mach 2 and the moon shots. They seemed to be sailing through the sky. Chugger went back to his seat. 'Going to feather the engines in rotation. Run a few tests.'

'As long as you don't get carried away.'

They began to strip the outer wrappings from the packets of leaflets.

'Reading,' shouted Chugger, jerking his thumb downwards. 'We used to formate here.'

'Sounds nasty. Right-oh. We'll heave some stuff out.'

When they'd done, Jarvis climbed up to admire the effect but the last of the shower of pamphlets had blown away like melting snowflakes. Reading was a blur of faint light below.

'Going to swing south-east and come in over the north. Miss the airport.' They were climbing again and beating an arc that swung them towards Essex. Then they were going down and Jarvis could see the great glittering collar of London flung down like the Crown Jewels, resolving itself into buildings and the flatly shining ribbon of the Thames. This must have been how it looked to the German bombers, he thought, only not so bright. Down there somewhere was Thaxsted Street. They began to stuff the leaflets out in furious handfuls, ripping open the rest of the packets and feeding them down the chute while the dark shape lumbered steadily on.

'Bombs gone,' Jarvis shouted. 'Let's get out of here.' He had a quick vision of pilots scrambling into their jets to intercept them. Suppose they mistook the old kite for a Russian. He didn't imagine the air training schools bothered much with Lancaster recognition these days. It was all right for Pilot Officer Prune & Co. up the front there. Nothing would suit them better than to go down in a glorious blaze but Jarvis wanted to live. 'One eye, one arm and one ambition', that was his Nelson touch and no 'Kiss me, Hardy' for a long time yet. They were over darkness again, the anonymity of fields. In the morning the streets would be seeded with AHIAR's words. He remembered a line they'd learnt at School: 'When men were all asleep the snow came flying,' and saw the big regular paper flakes drifting down with their message. 'Prepare to land,' Chugger broke in on his falling dream.

'Please God, let them remember how to get the bleeding

thing back on the earth.' Fortunately he couldn't see the ground rushing up at them, only feel the thump as they touched and the runway tearing off under their wheels like railway track beneath the Flying Scot. Then they were taxiing towards the hangar.

'Well, that's her outing for a bit,' Chugger said regretfully as they climbed down. 'In the morning we'll whip a couple of the engines out of her and yank her up to the roof. Spray her with a bit of dust and she'll look as if she's never moved. Never mind, old girl, it's better than the scrapheap. Tell Lottie we had a wizard time.'

'Thanks for the lift.'

'Any time you can afford it, old boy. Just say the word.'

'Take these,' Philomela said handing him a small brown bottle rattling with miniscule bombs.

'What will they do to me?'

'Turn you black, we hope.'

'Come again?'

'Don't you want to be so your own mother wouldn't know you?'

'Do you reckon they'll work?' Chuff looked doubtfully at the capsule in his hand.

'They've been used by civil rights workers in America to find out what happens to you if you're black. With the tan you've got already they should work quite quickly.'

'Dr Williams,' pink pills for pale people. You're probably right about me own mother. But what about the eyes? The blue-eyed Kaffir strikes again.'

'Dark glasses.'

'All I'll need is a fez to look like King Farouk. Would you say I was worth me weight in gold?'

'I think you'd better be Indian or perhaps Pakistani, then you could wear a Nehru hat. It'd be easier to manage than a turban.'

'And a Peter Sellers accent. Oh yes. Well I always wanted to be Sabu. What's the cover story?'

'You're a visiting researcher in tissue culture. Here are some books and pamphlets.'

'You want me to bone up on it? Black's medical dictionary as well.' He hefted the big red book.

'I'm worried Chuff. I feel time's suddenly run out. I want us to be ready for whatever is going to happen.'

'You didn't ever think we'd win, did you?'

'Not win, no, I knew we wouldn't do that. It takes years. Look how long the slave trade went on. But now that the papers have really taken us up with the leaflet drop, the authorities will have to try to find us. And after the next one . . .'

'What is the next one?'

'Right in the centre of London. Smithfield itself.'

'The major's policy of escalation. He's certainly got it all worked out, I'll say that for him. He should have been a general. They'll know of course where to begin looking. They've got files on all organizations. Now they understand the aims it's only a matter of feeding the information into the Manchester computer and waiting for it to spit out the right names. Do they realize, the princess and the rest?'

'I think they're deliberately not looking.'

'I've got something for you.' Jarvis went to the drawer where he had put the strange gun under the pyjamas he couldn't think of as his and took it out. 'What's this?'

Philomela put out a hand. 'It's a captive bolt pistol, sometimes known as a humane killer. It doesn't usually kill though. It's used to stun before cutting an animal's throat. Where did you get it?'

'I picked it up in Surefoods when you were trapped in the bloody cold store. I had some idea of shooting the door down.'

'The bolt only comes out a couple of inches; then you push it back again for the next shot.'

'So it wouldn't have been any use.' Jarvis put it back in the drawer.

'Do you think you should keep it?'

'Well I'm not going knocking on the bloody door to give it back. By the way, I'll need a passport to go with me black face.'

'Yes,' she said, 'we've thought of that.'

'I'd be a real laugh if I got deported for illegal entry.'

After the meal he was learning to call lunch, Chuff set himself to study. First he looked in the mirror to see if the pills were taking yet, but his skin was still tanned rather than dusky. A pity, he thought; his biological researches might have registered better on Dr Ali Barber than on Jarvis Chuff. He picked up *Alternative Methods to the Use of Animals in Bio-medical Studies* and began to read.

Philomela had taken the princess out in the car. The house was very quiet. Chuff's thoughts ambled from the multiplying sheets of cells. Somehow he ought to see Madeleine. If Philomela was right and the sky was going to fall he should make some arrangements. He daren't write to her direct. They might be vetting her post in wait for him to do just that. But he could send a note to his brother-in-law at work, marked personal. AHIAR could have it posted outside London. They couldn't still be watching Madeleine all the time. He hoped Philomela would understand, though when he got down to it he didn't really understand himself why he felt he had to see her or what he'd say when he did.

The sound of steps on the path below his open window made him put down his book and cross the room to look out. The path led on towards the shrubbery and the chapel. Chuff peered down. Unaware that he was being watched Raphael was taking a quiet saunter in the afternoon sun which baked the crazy paving and shimmered on the distant foliage draining the leaves to silver-grey. Yet Raphael moved as if it was winter, shoulders hunched, his hands behind his back with hands tucked in to opposite sleeves. The spruce priest was gone and in his place shuffled a maimed and weary black beetle. Jarvis watched him out of sight into the bushes and went back to the endless self-propagations of cell *y*. *In vitro* and *in vivo* were the key terms. Here he was *in vitro* behind glass, so to speak, and when Philomela came back he would be *in vivo*, the living warm suffering flesh capable of anything. All his life he had been the subject of experiment, bottled up in institutions, more dead than alive, largely unfeeling since he'd withdrawn himself from all that. Now with a gentle scalpel she had opened his chest and massaged his heart into beating. But he wasn't complaining. It was his choice, and yet not his choice, since he didn't seem to be able to help himself. Chance was indeed a fine thing as his mother had said, commenting on Kingdom never come, and Chuff felt that for the first time he was being given his.

The terms were meant to obscure with their dog-Latin that the things that suffered were really alive. There was so little difference between them to the ear, just a couple of letters, that you could easily mistake one for the other. The rabbits he remembered in their coffin boxes had been almost *in vitro* already with only the turning heads to remind you that they still lived. As their blindfolded eyes twitched, villagers ran with streaming faces from the flung gas cylinders and the birds fell dying out of the trees. It became a cause and effect from which there was no way out until by habit people believed it had become a necessity, like slavery and lopping off hands for theft. But there had been a way out to those and there could be to this, he was bloody sure, once the chain was broken. Usually he didn't have tea but now he wished Philomela would come back so they could sit in the drawing room with the french windows open and he could look at her coolly and sanely eating strawberries and cream. He wondered how long before his mother wouldn't know him and fought down a bout of panic, that he might be changed already and Philomela not recognize him, till the mirror reassured him. Maybe it would be gradual like growing old gracefully so those who saw him every day wouldn't notice at all. He began the section on the gas chromatograph. It wasn't strictly his field as a tissue culture expert, but he ought to know something about it.

'I don't even know why I bloody well have to see her and I know it's a sodding nuisance but I just feel I must.' He was embarrassed and angry as he always was when he had to say sorry or please and thank you.

'We'll tell her to bring her cat to the vet,' Philomela had said.

'What if she hasn't got one? I can't remember.'

'Then she'll have to use some of the family invention.'

So here he was now all done up in a white coat in a bare consulting room where the real vet had left him. Chuff wondered what old bull he'd been given about why this no doubt illegal immigrant had to meet a married woman clandestinely. It had been his first chance to try out his new disguise, accent and all. After several days on the red capsules his skin had deepened its colour to twilight. His little black toothbrush moustache gave him the touch of an anglophile Indian. He heard the handle turn and saw the door open a wedge in which Madeleine's face appeared puzzled and a little frightened.

'Excuse me.' She began to narrow the wedge.

'Madeleine. It's all right. It's Jarvey.' The door opened and she stared at him. 'Shut the bleeding door, for Christ's sake.'

'Now I believe it's you.' She came in, closing the door, and put a cat basket on the table. 'We haven't got a cat: they leave their hairs about, but the children keep this tortoise in the garden. I had a terrible job finding him. Once he wakes up there's no knowing where he might get to. Ian didn't like you writing. He thought you'd left the country.'

'Lost to sight, to memory dear, I know. Well, I'll be gone soon.' He knew now why he had wanted to see her. 'It's about the house. You said you'd found someone for it.'

'They didn't stay. There was no peace. The police were always cruising up and down, watching for you to come back. A couple of times they knocked them up and questioned them. That was when he decided to emigrate. It's empty now. I go in once a week to give eye to it a bit.'

'When I'm gone I want you to sell it. You can have the money. Put it aside for the kids or do what you like with it. Have you got a spare key?'

She opened her handbag and took out a small bunch on a ring including the big black latchkey he knew so well. 'I'll send you a letter from wherever I've gone giving you legal right to sell. Unless, of course, you'd rather keep it to let.'

'I'd rather sell. I'll tell you something: I always hated that house.'

'It's best if you sell it then.'

'It's too dangerous for you to go there.'

He looked at her hard. She wasn't daft. 'It's all right, no one will ever know if I've been. After all you didn't know me and blood's supposed to be thicker than water.' He shut the lid of the basket. 'You can take him home now, if it is a him. You ought to get a dog. They're company and good for the kids and a lot of kudos if you get the right sort.'

'Shall I be seeing you again?'

'Maybe one day when you're taking your holidays abroad.'

'Won't you never come back?'

'Never's a long time.'

He meant what he said about the dog. As Dr Ali Barber drove away he decided that it was their only chance for some warmth and disorder in their lives.

'Right,' Chuff said, 'we'll go through it all again 'cos this is the dodgiest one of all. At nine thirty the lads will come down Long Lane with their truck and begin fencing off the back with their signs and rubber bollards. If they're asked they're just paid to do a job, students on casual labour.'

'Which is what they are,' Philomela said, 'but students with a bias.'

'Some bleeding cherubs, I bet, with beards and hair down to their backsides.'

'Well the long hair's traditional for angels but I've never seen one with a beard it's true.'

'As soon as they're done, they drive off, which should mean they're all clear by the time I arrive at a quarter to ten. If I see everything's going nicely I get on with my bit but if anything's gone adrift we call it all off and a message goes to the hairy cherubs to pick up their stuff again. All being well, I should be finished by ten. As soon as I come past you you get going to get that silly beefeater with his fallen arches away from the front . . .'

They had rehearsed it carefully on the same night a week before and without the props. Now Chuff glanced at his watch, luminous beside the steering wheel as he drove the van up St John Street and into the avenue. The single policeman shifted his weight from one foot to the other and then was out of sight as Jarvis entered the arcade between the old and new markets. In a few seconds he was out the other side. He drew up in the deserted circus, barricaded now by the signs and diversions of the Purbeck Restoration Company, Buildings Renovated, whose van he was driving.

The angels of destruction had done well. The ladder was propped against the wall at exactly the right point. Pricking the city night sky the black cupolas of the old market stood up bold and squat. Chuff took his box of tricks and climbed with one hand. The jutting fringe of ornamental overhang looked as if it might let a foot through. Away to the right behind him was the lit bulk of St Bart's and a long gob would land in the Old Bailey. For a moment Chuff wished that could go as well, renovated by the Purbeck Restoration team. A ridge of stone coping helped him over the crumbling tile skirt.

He made for the furthest pepper-pot corner, set the small device, scurried to the next, then lowered the biggest pack through a skylight down into the heart of the building. On the way back he took in the third corner, skirted the overhang and began to climb down. The whole thing had taken less than ten minutes. He switched on the engine, turned the van and drove back through the alley and into St John Street. The blue-black shape of the policeman was still inked in in front of the far gates. Chuff passed Philomela in the uniform of a Bart's nurse but made no sign. It was important she shouldn't be suspected. He drew up after a left turn into Cowcross Street where he could see back the way he had come.

Now she would be telling the copper about the collapsed figure and asking him to help. Perhaps he would radio through to his station. They would cross the road, Philomela talking just enough. There was a flicker of movement in the driving mirror. They had entered the end of the street. Chuff let them take two steps before he pressed the button. There was a heartbeat's pause and then an explosion that shook the windscreen even where he sat. A burst of smoke gusted into the street. Philomela and the policeman flattened against a wall seemed stunned by the blast and unable to move, but after a few words they both set off towards the market. Philomela, he knew, would continue on to the hospital.

Chuff ditched the van in a narrow turning, picked up the

waiting car in Turnmill Street, drove down Farringdon Road, through Snow Hill and Cock Lane to the Hospital gates, where Philomela got in beside him. As they entered the empty darkness of the Old Bailey she unpinned her cap and let her hair loose. Jarvis took them through the entry to the North Circular.

'How did it look?' he asked.

'There aren't any words. Anything you can think of isn't enough. It was like the blitz all over again.'

'We're sure there wasn't anyone inside?'

'That's what the policeman said. "Thank Christ there was no one inside."'

'We'd best get back as quick as we can before someone comes calling.'

'Jarvis.'

'What?'

'Don't mention it to Aunt Lottie or the others, that the curtain's coming down.'

'You think they might want to make some last death-or-glory stand?'

'That's what I'm afraid of. I don't know quite what's going to happen but you must get out safely somehow.'

'I'm not going without you.' To his sudden terror she didn't answer.

But for the next few days nothing happened. They want us to hold our breath, Jarvis thought, so when they do come we choke on our words. The bombing of Smithfield had achieved the usual nine days notoriety. Police chiefs were interviewed, MPs had their say, several action groups tried to claim it for their own. It had been too easy, and where could they go next? What was bigger or would draw more limelight? He tried to predict the next move and failed. They could only repeat themselves until something went wrong and someone was hurt. Each job had had its moment of danger, its sacrifice. There had been the man at the window with the gun and the mink that would never make it in wild freedom but be trapped or hunted or starve perished with the cold. There had been the animals in their cages he had turned his eyes away from and there had been Philomela choking and burning. He waited in dread for the next victim.

They held a council of war after dinner three days later. The press had gone dumb; the bombing edged out by hotter news. At first the angels had been elated by the photographs of their success, now as Jarvis looked from one to the other he could see only his own uncertainty reflected.

'We must analyse the situation,' the major began, 'and decide on our next move.'

'We seem, if I may say so,' murmured Raphael, 'to have reached somewhat of an impasse.'

'They aren't taking us seriously is what you mean.' Chuff had never heard Althea speak out like this.

'Precisely.'

'Why not?' her gruff voice demanded.

Chuff shifted his feet. 'Gabriel?' He had been given permission to speak.

'Because they never take notice till people get killed and not even then. They won't even fence off the railway lines until kids are run over or electrocuted.'

'Philomela?'

'What Jarvis says is true, I'm afraid. There are certain built-in regulators in our society that make any form of change very difficult. There's the inertia of the status quo to be overcome. You have to get people to make an imaginative leap, to visualize how things could be different and that's very difficult because they're afraid of losing what they already have in the process. Then there's the wastage principle. We're prepared to have waste of all sorts, including lives, to keep the body of society going. It's a kind of anthropomorphism. We think of society as a real body. A healthy body has waste it gets rid of and society does the same. This makes us able to accept imprisonment and death as inevitable to society – for others of course.'

'I'm afraid it's all beyond my powers, dear,' the princess said. 'I do know, though, that they're hardening their hearts, like Pharaoh, you see.' Chuff wondered which of the plagues of Egypt he qualified as. His mother had often said he was worse than all of them rolled into one.

'So we have no choice but to go on. They think we're cranks

and that means either that we don't mean what we say or that what we say isn't reasonable. But we do mean it, by God, and we've given them reason enough. Our next move must be against government itself in its support for the status quo.' Oh gawd, Chuff thought, Guy Fawkes again. 'We shall burn down the Ministry of Agriculture,' the major concluded.

Desperately Jarvis tried to catch Philomela's eye but she was examining her mulberry-varnished fingernails with great concentration. 'Just where is it?' Jarvis asked.

'They have a department in Whitehall Place and offices in Horseferry Road. Perhaps we should take them together.'

'He's off his loaf,' Jarvis said to Philomela at the top of the stairs.

'Not quite, yet. It's despair and frustration. It's what happens when people can't see any way out.'

'He can't do it. There'll be soldiers and cops and Christ knows what. It may be booby-trapped in advance. That's what I'd do in their place if I knew what we were up to.'

'One of the built-in regulators I didn't mention was complacency. They won't think of it or think we'd dare.'

'And if we do that bugger, there'll just be another and another. Can't you see?'

'Yes,' Philomela said, 'I can see perfectly. That's why I'm afraid.'

It was a long time before he could get to sleep that night and when he did it was to start awake from dreaming that he had set a bomb in the house in Thaxsted Street and the walls were crumbling, the floors tilting as he clung to the window-sill inside. The boards slid away, leaving his feet to kick in the air and his arms cracked with the ache that would finally drop him into nothing.

Chuff got out of bed and went to the window. The night was moonless, warm and scented through the part-open window. Tobacco plants grew in the beds below and their cheap sweet smell carried memories of his father's gritty garden. It was still early. He tried to see how dark his hands had become against the window but there wasn't enough light even for that. More than anything he wanted Philomela. Was she asleep? He listened hard for her breathing but the walls were too thick. Maybe she was awake too. He picked up the short dressing gown and put it on. Barefoot he crossed the room, inched open his door and stepped outside. Like the thief he was, he put a hand on her doorknob and turned it.

'Are you asleep?'

'No.' There was a movement from the bed.

'I've come to steal.'

'Is it something I don't want you to have?'

Now his eyes were adjusted to the dark he could see her bare shoulders above the clothes. Against the shadows they glimmered cool and white. He drew back the sheet and looked down at her, naked because of the warm night. Then he bent his head and began to run his tongue over the warm ivory flesh. He felt her pull the dressing gown from his own shoulders. Still he lipped at the curving domes of breast and belly until she murmured indistinctly, pushed away the last folds of dressing gown and drew him down on top of her.

They came the next morning. Chuff saw the car swish to a halt as he was coming down the hall stairs, turned and ran up again to assume the rest of Dr Ali and came down his face composed, his chin sunk a little against his mandarin collar, plumping himself out like a winter sparrow in the cold. He could have stayed upstairs. They probably wouldn't have a warrant but it was better to establish his identity and anyway he wanted to know first-hand what was said. There were overtones that only his practised antennae might pick up.

At the drawing room door he paused a moment and bowed a little over his hands. 'I am so sorry, madame, you are having visitors. Please excuse me.' Dr Ali turned to go.

'Oh, do come in, Doctor. These gentlemen are just going. Dr Mehmad is a distinguished lecturer in tissue culture from Kashmir.' Lottie Shoe was taking the stage again.

'You are too kind.' He mustn't overplay it.

'You understand our position, madam,' the plainclothes senior was saying. 'We have to see everyone.'

'Of course you do. Even those who are a little old to be revolutionaries,' Lottie Shoe charmed him.

'It would be a great pity if people like yourself who had done such good work for charity should be foolish enough to get themselves involved in what might seem quixotic but may even be treasonable, certainly very dangerous.' Chatty, Chuff thought, his face orientally impassive but polite, therefore sharp. 'Law and order have to be maintained and actions like this are a menace to the fabric of society.' The riot act, that was what he was reading now and well into his stride. 'They may be used as cover for foreign-inspired agitators or ordinary criminals. I'm sure I don't have to tell you how undesirable that is.' His glance roamed round the furnishings, pricing the way of life they embodied. 'How long will you be staying, sir?' He swung round on Dr Ali Mehmad.

'Perhaps three weeks. It is very difficult for me to say how long.'

'You have your passport, sir?'

Chuff patted his pocket. 'They are upstairs. In Britain I do not always carry them on my person. I will bring them to you.' He turned towards the door.

'That won't be necessary, sir, thank you, but I'd advise you to carry them with you. This country isn't what it used to be.' He looked back at Lottie. 'If you know anyone, madam, that you think might be involved in this business it is of course your duty to inform the police. At the same time if you see it appealing to any young hotheads you'd be doing them a service if you warned them off. It carries a very long sentence and martyrdom can be very unglamorous.'

'As animals know, Inspector.'

'I beg your pardon, madam?' Chuff felt every nerve begin to hum its warning signals.

'Animals are martyred every day in their thousands and nobody even notices.' The princess smiled. 'We don't want any more forgotten martyrs, do we? After all, we are animals too.'

'Yes, well, that's a matter of opinion. Certainly some of us behave like it.'

'On the contrary, we are animals that behave like men; we invent bombs.'

The policeman shifted uncomfortably. 'Well, as I say, that's a matter for discussion. However, I think I've made myself clear. Good morning, madam.' He nodded to the rest of them in turn.

'I'll show you out, Inspector,' Philomela said.

'Father Raphael, I wonder if you would be so good,' Lottie said clearly above the noise of their exit.

'Certainly, Princess. Now what can I get you?'

'I think perhaps a little pre-lunch drink. A gin and lime for me for old time's sake.' They heard the door close and, a minute after, the slamming of car doors and the engine firing. 'Lunch will be ready very soon I've no doubt. Ah, here's Philomela.'

'They've gone.'

The princess sat down with a sigh of relief. 'My dears, how was I?'

'You were absolutely marvellous,' Philomela said.

'I thought I had better show a little spirit or they would be suspicious. Was that right?'

'You had me a bit hot under the collar at first,' Chuff said, 'but once I realized what you were up to I saw it was the right thing. If we'd all been too smarmy they'd have smelt something.'

'You almost frightened me, dear boy,' Raphael said. 'That disguise is really most professional. I found I'd forgotten what you actually looked like.'

'Did I miss much?'

'Only the opening rounds,' Philomela answered. 'What do you think? Did they guess anything?'

'Can't be sure. We got the standard lecture. They'd find it hard to believe of Lottie. I'd say they haven't got anything to go on yet, just routine checks. But his eyes were everywhere and he's no fool. They'll be back.'

'Even if they search there's nothing to find,' Raphael said, but Jarvis thought he could hear a tremor of doubt in his voice. Suddenly he remembered the pistol under the pyjamas in his drawer. That was one thing. What also might there be? You were never quite safe. Suppose they were to analyse the pills Chuff was taking. Could they tell what they were for from the components and penetrate his black skin?

'There must be records of the cherubs. Could they find those?'

'I don't think so,' Lottie said. 'All the same perhaps I should ring Althea and Alex and let them know what's happened.'

'The phone may be bugged,' Chuff said.

'I thought you needed a very special order for that?' Raphael queried.

'This could be a national emergency: they'd get an order quick enough if they wanted one.'

'All the same,' Lottie said, 'if I'm careful I think I should try.' She picked up the receiver and dialled. 'Hello, Alex, how are you?' There was a pause while the receiver crackled and buzzed like a wasp in a cocoa tin. 'I don't understand. No, she's not here. What time? I'll get her to ring you. Goodbye . . . Or, just a minute, you ring me if you hear first.' She put down the receiver in its cradle and faced them with a look of bewilderment. 'Alex says they had visitors earlier this morning and then Althea rode over to see us, to warn us, I think he meant, but he's guessed the phone might not be safe as well.'

'What time?' Chuff demanded, as she had done.

'Over an hour ago. I don't understand.'

But Jarvis did. In a second he saw it. 'Stay there,' he said to Philomela, 'with Lottie.' She moved forward and then stopped, her eyes opening with sudden understanding.

'Philomela,' Lottie said, 'what is it?'

He ran through to the back of the house, yanked open the door and ran on again through the park. The sun pounced down on him. The air was still and heavy. His clothes soaked through with sweat and his breath rasped painfully in his chest as he pounded over the grass. At first when he reached the bottom he couldn't see what he was looking for and then he heard the soft snort of a horse from the other side of the hedge. Opening the gate he went through into the field beyond. It was all as he had expected, as dozens of westerns had taught him it would be: the hunched bundle of sticks and old clothes lying at the foot of the hedge, its neck awry, and Delilah nosing at it gently.

As he approached, the horse reared up on its hind legs and beat its hooves at him, snorting angrily. It was quite right, Jarvis thought, he was an intruder. Delilah would never let him near. He must get someone she could trust. He turned and ran back the way he had come, ran, although it was clear from the position in which the bundle was lying, from its stillness, that time didn't matter any more. With a bit of his mind he noticed that the birds were silent again as if acknowledging the victim he had been waiting for. Outside the back door he took deep breaths and composed his sentences in his head.

'She's had an accident down by the hedge.'

'I'll come,' said Philomela.

'It has to be someone the horse trusts. She won't let me near her.'

Lottie stood up. 'I'll go. She's always good with me. We must hurry.'

'There's no need to hurry,' Chuff said. 'I'm sorry.'

Delilah had let Lottie take her dangling reins and lead her away while Jarvis and Philomela picked up Althea's small crumpled shape that was already cold and stiffening in spite of the sun. Raphael had stopped behind to telephone for a doctor and to tell the major. Philomela checked for a pulse but it was clear that Althea had been dead for some time. She had died instantly, Jarvis hoped and thought. The small procession through the sweltering park was both macabre and ridiculous. Jarvis looked ahead at Delilah. Had Althea deliberately jumped at the hedge because she was in a hurry to warn them or had Delilah set herself at it and then stopped short? There was no way of knowing. The horse tossed its head and snorted nervously still, but there was no getting inside it for the truth. They were up against the barrier that foiled imagination. Between humans it was hard enough to surmise what went on in other heads but between human and non-human it became possible to believe that nothing went on in there at all. And if we found a species that could talk, if at last we understood what dolphins gossiped about and they would tell it to us, would we stop feeling that we were outside the animal kingdom, them and us, believe we were not alone with our terrible burden of intelligence that made us capable of monstrousness beyond the beasts and made us glory in our difference, would we learn in fact to love ourselves a bit?

*

'Privately in the Chapel of St Francis' the notice said in *The Times*. Chuff had never known anyone before who'd had their funeral announced to the nation. His mother's, and he supposed his father's too, had figured in the local paper and strangers had appeared to shake his hand and explain that they had sat in the same classroom as her or been workmates together when she was in her teens.

'If the peelers are suspicious they'll be at the cemetery. Keep your eyes skinned for them.'

'Aren't you coming?'

'I don't think Dr Mehmad would attend a Christian funeral somehow.'

'It'll be terrible. I always hate them, but I'll have to go to look after Aunt Lottie.'

'Raphael will be there, I suppose.'

'He's taking the service.'

Chuff opened his mouth and shut it on second thoughts. 'I could look in on the chapel bit,' he said. 'They can't gatecrash that.'

'Please,' she said. 'It'll help to think you're there.'

So now he stood at the back without Dr Mehmad's hat and listened as Raphael went through the motions for tucking the old girl decently underground. The major seemed so frail now that a puff of wind would carry him off. Lottie leaned hard against Philomela for support but when Raphael had said his piece about our sister and her concern for all living things she suddenly stepped forward and sat down at the organ. With a voice that grew more powerful as she went on she began to sing something that Chuff was sure wasn't a hymn.

'Thy hand, Belinda, darkness shades me,
On thy bosom let me rest.
More I would but death invades me,
Death is now a welcome guest.'

Then, the notes rising among the green pillars till he found himself looking up to see if faces were peering down from the rafters, she sang with all the resonance of that long-broken black shellac platter:

'When I am laid, am laid in earth,
May my wrongs create
No trouble in thy breast,
Remember me, but, ah, forget my fate.'

'Remember me,' the voice sobbed and begged until Chuff felt his eyes sting and the knot in his chest like a chunk of hard potato that wouldn't go down.

Five

'The bands are playing so gaily, so bravely, and one does so want to live.'

'You were right,' Philomela said when it was all over and they were home again and Lottie had gone to rest in her room. (There were no funeral baked meats, Jarvis noticed, no obligation to provide plates of cold meat and salad, trifle and cups of tea with a nip in them while people sat round not knowing what to say.) 'They were there, skulking at the back.'

'Back of what?'

'There were a lot of people, men and women who'd worked for her and others I didn't recognize.'

'Cherubs?' Jarvis frowned.

'They could have been. I don't know.'

'Enough to increase the flatfoot's suspicions?'

'I just don't know. Maybe.'

'Sod.' He looked out at the park that was drained of colour by an overcast sky. 'It's the end. They must see it's the bloody end.'

'At the moment they're too shaken to see anything. You knew it would happen, didn't you?'

'Not what, but I felt something would come unstuck. We had it too easy over Smithfield.'

'Superstition?'

'Not exactly. More like the law of averages. The chance of it going wrong increases in proportion to the number of jobs you pull, like accidents with the number of cars on the road. You panic or you get careless and then you make a mistake.'

'What do we do?'

'I'm buggered if I know at this minute.'

Philomela went up to see how the princess was. In an effort to sort some order into the future Jarvis took the path through the shrubbery to the chapel. Somehow he couldn't face the park. He knew what he wanted and if he couldn't have it he might as well resign himself to the nick. Wherever he was without Philomela would be doing life behind his door. He pushed open the fortress gate to the chapel and went inside. The air was deathly with the smell of dying white flowers. Raphael flitted among them in his long black robe.

'Come in, dear boy. I was just tidying.'

Jarvis perched himself on the top of a pew. 'Is that the first you've done?'

Raphael paused with one hand full of a confetti of fallen petals. 'I don't quite . . .'

'The first burial.'

'Yes, indeed. Fortunately they don't arise too often.'

'No, they wouldn't in your situation. It's not as if it was like being a real vicar. I don't suppose they taught it in your college,' he went on harshly. 'I don't remember any classes being offered in how to take a funeral at Wandsworth. Mark you, it's a good few years since I was there; it might have been different in your day.'

'It was Durham,' Raphael said and sat down heavily.

'Why did you tell me you'd never been inside?'

'I thought if you knew that you'd realize, and I was right, wasn't I?' he smiled. 'How did you guess?'

'I saw you out of the window when you thought no one else was knocking about. You had the old lag's shuffle. You must have done a stretch to pick that up.'

'A one and a three with full remission.'

'Impersonation with attempt to defraud?' Raphael nodded. 'No little choirboys?'

'I liked them of course, but I didn't ever touch.'

'Seems a funny thing to lay claim to if it wasn't true.'

'But it was, in spirit. That was my real crime, not what I was convicted for.'

'And deceiving the princess?'

Raphael looked at the petals in his hand. 'She knows I've been to prison but not the truth of what for. You see I feel I am what I seem. If you wear the clothes it works its way inwards. There was never any chance when I was a boy. My father wanted me to follow him in insurance.'

'Couldn't you have done it later?'

'You have to say you have a vocation. I just want to be a vicar. It's not the same thing. Then once I'd been convicted it was impossible.' He pushed a petal boat across the pew seat. 'What are you going to do?'

Jarvis lowered himself from the back of the pew. 'Do, why should I do anything?'

'You won't tell the princess?'

'That'd be a nice present to make her at this moment wouldn't it? But if I ever find you've been duck-shoving her or upsetting her I shall break your bleeding neck.'

Raphael shuddered. 'Dear boy, you're so rough. Why should I hurt her: she believes in me. For her I am what I seem. At last, here, I have everything I want.'

'Except the choirboys.'

'Soon, mercifully, I shall be too old to want even them.'

'Don't bank on it,' Chuff said.

'Will you tell Philomela?'

'Later maybe. When this is all over.'

But it was clear when they met again that the major hadn't finished yet. 'We must go on now for Althea's sake,' he said, his hands on the stick trembling a little.

'No, Alex,' said the princess firmly. 'It is meant for a sign, a very terrible sign.'

'Nonsense, Althea was a casualty of war. She would have wanted us to go on. She was a Pheidippides or a dispatch rider who didn't get through. Even more I'm convinced we must strike at the very heart of those who were responsible.'

'You realize,' Chuff put in, 'it's next door to Scotland Yard.'

'All the more reason why they will be totally unsuspecting.'

The princess stood up. She was wearing a long black dress of several floating layers and her hair gleamed the fierce and brilliant white of an avenging angel. 'I absolutely forbid it. I feel in here,' she put a hand to her bosom, 'that it would be terribly wrong. You and I have nothing to lose, but these children,' Chuff felt his years slip away and almost looked down to see if his knees were scabbed, 'these children have a right to some kind of future.'

'It's a betrayal,' the major was on his feet too, 'of all we've worked for, and of Althea.'

'No one,' said the princess with dignity, 'loved her more than I did. I don't believe she would want a pointless sacrifice as a memorial.'

The major marched from the room like a veteran on Armistice Day. Lottie Shoe sighed. 'Of course he's upset,' she said. 'We all are. My dears, you must go. I feel that very strongly.'

'There were plainclothes men at Althea's funeral,' Philomela said.

'Yes,' the princess sighed. 'I saw them. I did think . . . However, that isn't important. What is important is that Jarvis should get away.'

'I'm not going without Philomela.'

'And you, I suppose, think I can't be left alone,' Lottie said. 'Now really, all this must stop. There's nothing to connect me with anything, except you two. I shall be perfectly safe. I've done nothing except harbour an escaped convict and if he's not here it can't be proved that he ever was or indeed that I knew who he was. Nor . . .' a plump white hand silenced Philomela, 'can it be proved that a distinguished old lady like me was an accessory before and after to her niece's doings. I shall make all the arrangements for you both to go. Alex isn't the only one with organizing ability. Your money,' she turned to Jarvis, 'is already taken care of. Althea did it.' For a moment her voice choked. 'One thing Alex hasn't thought of is that he no longer has a fighting fund. Apart from leaving him enough to live on, and various small bequests, all the rest of her money goes to found a scholarship for research into animal contraceptives.'

'There's something I have to get over with before I can go,' Jarvis said when they were alone. 'I've got to see something.'

'All right,' said Philomela, 'when do we go?'

'You don't have to come with me.'

'Would you rather I didn't?'

'No. It's not that. I'd much rather you did.'

'That's settled then.'

'There's one or two things I'll need. Can you get me a needle and cotton?'

Out of a large handkerchief Chuff stitched a shoulder holster for the strange pistol. To leave it behind when the fuzz might come with a search warrant was to endanger the princess's innocence. To take it with him was to risk his own but that seemed preferable. He could always ditch it in a sticky moment or so he hoped. But it was bulky and too obvious to carry in a pocket. He'd tried and it stuck out like a hard on. There was an old gag of Mae West's: 'Is that your gun, officer, or are you glad to see me?' that about covered it and made him laugh even as he pricked blood on to the holster from his finger.

Philomela had provided them with an authentic agent's letter to view and a tag for the heavy latchkey. He knew as he put it into the lock why he had asked Madeleine for the key. To use any other on his own front door would have been a kind of rape. Dr Mehmad and his secretary were looking over a house in one of the last corners of London that was still cheap. They had cruised up Thaxsted Street once in the taxi and had left it round the corner. Now they turned on foot into the road, deserted except for one middle-aged woman sweeping her front. Jarvis grinned to himself. He knew her, had done for years, but she would never look for him behind Dr Mehmad's glasses. She was late doing her front: she always was. 'Girl Tullis is proper slummocky,' his mother whispered. The green tissue-paper rounds of the polled elm leaves were thickening with summer grime. From the far end of the road came the tank rumble and crash of a bulldozer. Chuff peered up the street trying to penetrate the cloud of dust where the derelict frames of other identical houses were being levelled. The whole area seemed to be coming down.

'This is where I was born,' he said.

'Yes,' said Philomela. 'I know.'

The passage smelt dark and damp but then it always had after the street, particularly in summer when the old bricks gave off their own peculiar smell. Or perhaps it was the mortar.

Chuff wouldn't have put it past the blokes who had run this lot up for next to nothing to have used quicklime if it was cheaper.

They went through the rooms one after the other where all was just as he'd left it like the Sleeping Beauty's castle. Only the clocks had stopped and he couldn't remember if that had been so in the story. Time had gone on outside, but what about inside? Dust settled, their beards and hair grew like the hedge that hid them but they didn't age. The clocks must have stopped. He wound the front room one that had been their wedding present, in its varnished wooden case, shaped like a bowler hat whose brim had uncurled in the rain, and set it to the right time. The house was smaller and darker than he remembered it as if he'd only been a child there. There was a light sandy dust on the steps of the crenellated beige tile fireplace that had seeped in from the demolition.

Jarvis led the way through the scullery to the backyard. It had run wild. The lawn was kneehigh in places with dandelion clocks puffing their gossamer parachutes into the air. The rambler rioted over the fence. Chuff tore off a white papery rose and gave it to her, a heavy damp head sinking in the green glossy foliage. He pinched the soot from his fingers. Where was the burnt-out stub of saucepan now?

They went back into the house and climbed the stairs. He wanted to take something with him but he wasn't sure what it should be. Most things were too unwieldy. He would have liked the big old brown teapot but that would have been ridiculous. All at once he knew another reason why he had come. 'I wanted you to see.'

'Yes,' said Philomela again, without impatience, 'I know.'

Madeleine, or someone, he supposed it must be her, had stripped the house of all small movables that might have gone into a pocket. 'This was my bedroom,' he said turning the handle. He imagined a faint whiff of burnt fivers. The young marrieds had obviously left it very much to itself. In the corner stood his mother's tin trunk, locked. The bed was stripped to the mattress. Taking out his bunch of keys he unlocked the trunk and laid back the lid. This was where Madeleine had buried the mammicks. Chuff lifted them out: small ornaments stamped with names of seaside towns, bundles of their school reports, their last ration books, his mother's Co-op card, birth certificates, marriages, deaths, one or two rings and brooches, a necklace of jet beads, and photographs, studio portraits and snaps together. He lifted out a large head of himself smiling gormlessly. If it had been taken the other end you'd have seen the cradle marks, Jarvis thought. Hardly knowing what he did he took the pistol from its handkerchief sling and holding it against the glass above the bridge of the nose, in mid-forehead between the eyes, he slipped the safety catch and pulled the trigger.

There was a tremendous bang that flung his hand back from the shattered picture, a small cry from Philomela and the splintering of glass and wood.

'Why?' she said, stepping forward.

'He's weak and stupid and I hate him.'

'You mustn't,' she said. 'I don't.'

'I can't find anything to take.'

'There's no need. Nothing's lost that has been and you're not betraying anything. It's all part of you.' She picked the long splinters of glass from the stunned head and handed it to him. Chuff put the things back into the trunk and then, as an afterthought, the pistol with its bolt sticking out. Madeleine could store it for a bit and then, maybe, ship it out to him wherever he was going. He relocked the trunk and pulled it over the neat round hole in the lino and floorboard where the bolt had gone in. The splinters of glass he wrapped in an old tablecloth and hid under the mattress. Philomela picked up the rose. In the wardrobe he remembered there was that old coat of his mother's. The lapel was capped with the head of a pin.

'See a pin and pick it up/All the day you'll have good luck,' she muttered as she bent triumphantly over the small sword glinting on the pavement. Jarvis pinned the rose to Philomela's coat. There was nothing else he needed to take.

'Your flight is at eleven forty on Air India,' the princess said. 'So we can have an early dinner, then you can drive to the airport. Leave the car in the park, put the ticket in this envelope and drop it in the post box. Then I can get someone to pick it up later. It's a great pity I can't drive any more.' They knew she was thinking of Althea.

'Aunt Lottie,' Philomela said, 'will you truly be all right?'

'You're not to give it a moment's worry. Jarvis, you see that she doesn't. I shall be perfectly all right although it will be rather quiet at first. But there's lots to do. I've decided I've been rather too retiring in the past. I shall go to more things, talk to more people, work even harder to convince them. Instead of disbanding All Heaven In A Rage I think we should, as the Americans say, make them over, change the name but keep the organization, if you see what I mean. I've been trying over a few in my head. How does NSUS strike you? Nature's Social Union Society.'

'"I'm truly sorry man's dominion/Has broken nature's social union"?' Philomela said. 'It should be popular with the Scottish branch but the initials sound too like . . .' The telephone rang sharply into her words.

'Take it for me, dear.'

Philomela lifted the receiver. 'It's Mr Billings,' she said, holding it out towards the princess. 'He says he has a message for you. I think you'd better speak to him.'

The princess took the telephone. 'Yes, Mr Billings? How is Major Cracknell?' There was a pause while she listened. Chuff was aware of Philomela breathing a little quickly, 'short thick pants' he remembered, and then the sudden change in Lottie's expression and his own head beginning to buzz with tension. 'What time did he go?' the princess asked. They watched her hear the answer, say thank you to the voice on the line and put down the receiver.

'Who's Billings?' asked Chuff.

'Alex's batman. What is it?' Philomela asked Lottie.

'He sent a message to say he was going ahead.'

'You mean the silly old sod's going it alone?'

'I think that's what it means,' the princess nodded.

'Gawd and all his angels,' Chuff exploded, 'that means the ministry.'

'He left an hour ago.'

'We'll have to try to stop him,' said Chuff. Philomela was already moving towards the door.

*

They fled up the M4 on the limit. As they passed the lights of Heathrow a jet rose flashing into the night. Ruefully Chuff wondered if they would be back in time to follow it.

'No messing about,' he said, 'I'm going straight up Whitehall.' At Knightsbridge it was already twenty past nine. The car wove round Hyde Park Corner and into St James's Park. 'Nobody at home,' Chuff said as they passed the Palace. 'The Queen Mum's got a few friends in for the evening.' Dark limousines were disgorging distinguished elderly couples in evening dress in the Mall. He turned down Horse Guard's Parade, left into Parliament Square and left again up Whitehall.

As they neared the Cenotaph they realized they were too late by the crowds and fire engines. Chuff took the first turning alongside the War Office. 'Whitehall Place'll be sealed off, but we might get through this way.' A narrow street let them see through to the ministry building. Smoke was pouring from it. They left the car behind and hurried forward, Lottie almost carried between the other two. Firemen had run ladders to the upper windows, and even as they watched a man was helped down while a second palely anonymous face appeared like a Hallowe'en turnip lantern through the smoke above.

'Where do you think Alex is, inside?' Lottie clutched Chuff's arm.

'No,' said Chuff, 'he's not. He's setting fire to the other bugger while they're busy there. That's what we planned.' He turned and led them back to the car. Halfway there Lottie stumbled. 'Bandychair,' said Jarvis, reaching for Philomela's hands. Together they trotted her up the street.

Jarvis swung the car into the Embankment, past the Houses of Parliament and towards Lambeth Bridge. At the roundabout he swerved into Horseferry Road, almost deserted under its lamps. Philomela sighed with relief. 'At least he hasn't done it yet.'

'No, but where the hell is he?'

They drew up outside Great Westminster House. 'Another picture palace,' said Chuff. 'It's bloody enormous. He could be anywhere in there. Sit tight. I'm going over for a look.' The foyer was quite dark. The big swing doors had closed notices on them. Chuff pushed first one, then another. The third moved under his touch. Now he was sure Alex was inside. He slipped through the door.

It was so quiet he might have been rifling a tomb. Chuff stood still a moment to let his villain's reflexes come into play. Beyond the foyer he saw the doors of a lift. A faint movement caught his attention; the arrow of the floor indicator was rising slowly like a fish in a tank going up for food. He watched it till it surfaced three floors above. Give him time to get out, bring the lift down, step into it, press the button. Was the old boy armed? Had he really gone bonkers and would shoot on sight? Jarvis crossed his fingers. The lift doors opened automatically, exposing him in a lit frame but the corridor he stepped into was dark and empty. The major might be in any one of the offices in this bureaucratic warren. Chuff began systematically opening each door enough for a quick look round. The fourth was a big room filled during the day with clerkly small fry, its windows looking on to the street below.

Silhouetted against one of them were the major's head and shoulders. He seemed to be staring down at the car. Chuff took three silent steps into the room. 'It's all right Alex; time to go home.' The figure swung round. At almost the same moment the lights were switched on from behind Chuff. He turned quickly. A man stood blinking in the doorway.

'Good evening' Dr Mehmad said. 'You are the caretaker here? I am Dr Mehmad. This gentleman is my patient. He is not well, you understand. Would you please help me get him to the car downstairs where his sister, poor lady, is waiting to take him home.'

'Well, I don't . . .' the caretaker began.

'He thinks that people are after him, you know, and so he tries to hide in empty buildings,' Chuff babbled, watching the man. 'If you would just go to the window you will see the motor car with ladies in it.'

The caretaker stood undecided. Could he hit him, Chuff wondered, if he had to? If he hadn't locked the pistol in the tin trunk he could have used it to frighten him. But at that moment while the man still hesitated there came a strange noise from the major. Briefly Chuff thought it might be an attack of some kind. Then he realized that the old man was choking in tears. 'You see,' Chuff said to the caretaker, 'how he is. Come now.' He put his hand on Alex's shoulder. 'Most sad.' Together they began to lead him to the door. 'Give me your briefcase, there's a good chap.'

The caretaker rang for the lift and they went down. Gradually the major grew quieter and cuffed the glistening tears from his cheeks. They helped him across the dark foyer. 'He must have found one door open,' Chuff said. 'He tries them all, you see.'

'I heard a bit of a noise and I said to the wife, I'll just take a look. You can't ever tell, seeing as how they so often work late, who's in and who's out.'

'You have been most helpful,' Chuff said as they stepped into the street. He was aware of the car door opening and Lottie's voice.

'Oh, Alex.'

'The lady would want you to have this.' He peeled a fiver from his wallet.

'Thank you very much, sir, and I hope he'll soon be better.'

'Yes, indeed,' Chuff said and got into the car.

'Where to?' asked Philomela when they were safe in the maze of streets behind Victoria.

'Will that bloke put two and two together when he sees the papers?' Jarvis wondered.

'I'm too old,' the major said, 'too old.'

'You need a complete rest,' Lottie announced firmly. 'Jarvis drop us at Paddington. I shall take you down to Theodora's for a fortnight.' She opened her handbag. 'Everything you need is in here.' She gave Jarvis a thick manilla envelope. 'Now step on it or you'll miss the plane.'

'Where's Theodora's?' Jarvis asked when they had left the others at the station. He was stowing the contents of the envelope in his pockets. There hadn't been time for lengthy farewells.

'It's a vegetarian guest house in Cornwall.'

'Will they be all right?'

'Theodora will give him an alibi. She's always been hazy about dates.'

Jarvis looked at the briefcase. 'What about that? We don't know what's in it. It could go off at any minute.'

'We'll take a quick detour to the Embankment and drop it off a bridge.'

The lights of Heathrow swam up at them for the second time that evening. There was still half an hour before their flight, though years had passed since they had seen the jet take off from the car windows. They left the Rover in the long-term parking lot and checked in the two suitcases they had hastily packed and flung into the boot. The charming Indian receptionist at the Air India desk smiled up at Dr Mehmad. Philomela took his arm. 'I think the sooner we get you back to your native colour the better,' she said.

While they waited for their flight to chatter into place on the indicator they wandered through the airport emporium with its last-minute temptations. Plastic dolphins swam smiling in the hot air currents above the stalls, ducks dabbled along the counter, a pink rabbit pricked its ears in a cellophane burrow. Bears and penguins jostled in the window. Jarvis picked up a bag full of farm animals. Noah led the couples into the ark on the first conservation trip. Their moulded features smiled with pleasure or were placidly vacant. Among the books kittens, puppies, hens, pigs and even mice played out the childish Never Never fantasies where no one was ever hurt or killed. Philomela bought two paperback thrillers. The numbers of their magic carpet went up on the tote. Jarvis's belly tightened as they separated at passport control. He joined the aliens queue.

With a sweating hand he put out Dr Mehmad's passport. 'I hope you had a pleasant stay,' the official said as he checked it.

'Oh yes, thank you, very nice indeed,' Jarvis offered. He was too old to hang for a lamb. He could see Philomela waiting beyond the barrier. The man slapped his passport shut and passed it back. Others were pressing at his heels. His legs trembled all the way across the hall and into the bus that took them across to the waiting plane. Saried attendants bowed them aboard. They fastened their seat belts and the plane joined the stream for take-off.

'Is it all right,' he asked suddenly, 'your coming with me?'

'Silly Chuff.'

'I hope nobody's thought to put a bomb on this plane.'

They began their run-up; the engines hurled them along the ground and up into the night sky. 'Chance,' his mother said in his ear, 'is a bloody fine thing.'

Afterword

When I first conceived *I Want to go to Moscow* in the early seventies, it was in a mood of fear and frustration. Glamourized by the student unrest of the late sixties, violence had suddenly become fashionable in seemingly radical circles. It hung almost palpably in the air, generating an intellectual tension akin to the physical excitement attendant on riot or the various forms of gang warfare. Ends were again being used to justify means: the Holy War for the Just Cause. It was hard in such an atmosphere to keep a footing against the thrust of energy that's always given off by a whiff of violence. The Gandhian principle of passive resistance suddenly seemed old-fashioned and attenuated beside the glamour of a Guevara, yet I felt that to be swept along was to abandon years of rational allegiance to both democracy and my own modified but strongly felt passivism.

This was the ethical problem which gave rise to the book but there was another closely entwined with it which was to provide its fictional dress. The report of the Littlewood Committee on animal welfare had by then gathered dust on the shelf for five years without even a Parliamentary debate. Vivisection had reached over five and a half million experiments a year in the UK and the industrialization of farming involved yet more millions of animals in miserable caged lives and early deaths as the consumer society grew yearly more voracious. For decades animal welfare campaigners had practised the democratic arts of leafletting, fund-raising, petitions and letters to Parliament and press against this background of worsening conditions.

Democracy is a creaking machine requiring constant adjustment and attention. Consensus is necessary to make it work at all and that is only achieved by sensitive tuning. When this fails and the seesaw of alternate change and consolidation in any given area becomes stuck, the frustration of those expectations which the system itself engenders, produces increasing disillusion which, in its most extreme form, may become sour and violent. It seemed to me that we were rapidly approaching this point in the struggle for changes in man's treatment of the other animals, and that when Parliament and democracy itself were perceived as being in a state of inertia an attempt would be made to move things on by direct action. The struggle for animal welfare would become a call for animal rights.

The cause, the defence of those unable to speak for themselves and to whom violence was being done every second of day and night, was not only one which I felt passionately about but which, short of human genocide, provided the strongest ethical grounds for the justification of extreme action, of the holy war. One one side was ranged the full weight and power of the establishment, both of government and big business, while on the other was a collective David of passionate but largely powerless individuals.

I wanted to write a novel of ideas but I didn't want it to be merely propaganda. I therefore cast it in the form of a picaresque caper with touches of Ealing Studios comedy, choosing a set of unremittingly English characters. However, a work of art should be at least as many layered as angel cake and so there are several other elements woven into the book's fabric. One of these, which reflects its central concern with the permanence of moral values and the attempt to hang on to the truth against the constant rewriting of history, is the metaphor of Moscow itself as the longed for ideal of *The Three Sisters*, incorporating our wartime and present attitudes to Russia and its massive cultural and political importance. For me nothing can expunge that wartime truth of Russia our ally against fascism, although this doesn't mean I am uncritical of much of communism's political practice. It's significant however, that for publication in the USA the book had to be retitled, and my homage to Chekov replaced by my deference to Blake as *All Heaven In A Rage*. Yet another aspect of the preservation of values and of a particular vision of the truth is expressed in the language Jarvis Chuff, the non-violent thief hero, uses and in which is embedded like strands of moss in the agate, the idioms and attitudes of my own childhood.

In *I Want to go to Moscow* I plotted an escalating campaign of protest, beginning with a jailbreak by helicopter which foreshadowed the use of the same device by the IRA the following year. The direct actions I envisaged in pursuit of animal rights, the freeing of animals from cage and laboratory, and the destruction of environments where they suffer and die, have become standard practice among animal liberationists. So too has the organization of cells of activists with an outer ring of support from many in the general welfare movement. I don't believe that the relationship between the book and subsequent actual events is one of cause and effect but rather that by the hypothesizing process, common to both scientists and artists but known among the latter as 'imagination', I was able, as writers often can, to predict possibilities inherent in the position that did indeed become fact. Correctly read, the novel's central message is anti-violence and pro both life and hope.

Twelve years later the Littlewood Report has still not been debated by Parliament but we are at last promised new legislation. It is now over a hundred years since the last comprehensive act dealing with our treatment of the other animals and in particular with vivisection. What is promised looks, as I write, too little, too late. The pro-vivisection, pro-hunting lobbies are as powerful and vociferous as ever but the general public has become increasingly uneasy about many aspects of how we treat our cousins. Now it isn't the elderly long standing campaigners whom, for affectionately comic purposes, I envisaged in the novel as the most ardent liberationists but young recruits disillusioned with more conventional politics and moved by a compassionate idealism. This nevertheless sometimes leads them into counter-productive acts on the edge of that violence I have tried in the novel to show the dangers and limitations of, as a morally justified form of political expression, however righteous the cause.

Whether we would have at last been promised parliamentary action without the activities of the Animal Liberation Front, as the extreme activist wing of the animal rights movement is called, is now impossible to say. At the very least they are a marker of the breadth and depth of concern felt across society which the growth of vegetarianism, the veal boycott, the public rejection of blood sports shown by opinion polls, the support for Green Peace and its anti-sealing activities all testify to.

The other day I heard a radio report from the annual conference of the American equivalent of the Royal Society, extolling the expediency of using human tissue culture for testing anti-cancer agents as against the blunt instrument of testing on other species. Ironically to some of us it was even suggested that it would be desirable to re-test all those substances which had only been tested on other animals. When I wrote the book, the use of tissue culture was a method still in its infancy and still dismissed as an adequate research tool by the medical establishment even though it had accurately raised doubts about the safety of thalidomide, doubts which were tragically ignored. It is, I believe, by the discovery and pro-motion of alternatives that animals will be phased out of laboratories and that is why in the novel the hero is ultimately disguised as a specialist in tissue culture.

As I've said elsewhere, the last bastion to succumb to reason will probably be the military. When you are contemplating, even in a war game, the killing of millions of your fellow humans, the use of other creatures in, shall we say, weapons testing hardly raises an ethical eyebow. Fortunately the public isn't always so rational and finds the thought of shot, irradiated and gassed monkeys and sheep in the simulation of war peculiarly repugnant. It is felt that in this respect at least we should keep our violence to ourselves. I have come full circle back to the proposition with which I began the book that the espousal of violence can only breed violence. Nothing since the writing of *I Want to go to Moscow* has caused me to change this position which I reiterated in the final chapter of my last novel *Londoners* where a mindless terrorist bombing supplied the modern parallel to the ultimate evil at the bottom of Dante's *Hell*. The mid-eighties seem a necessary moment to say it all again in this new edition against a background of national and international violence and overhung by the government's legislative intentions which, on past showing, will settle the fate of millions of sentient creatures for perhaps the next hundred years.

London July 1985